Love is
a time of enchantment:
in it all days are fair and all fields
green. Youth is blest by it,
old age made benign:
the eyes of love see
roses blooming in December,
and sunshine through rain. Verily
is the time of true-love
a time of enchantment — and
Oh! how eager is woman
to be bewitched!

SET THE STARS ALIGHT

Beautiful Gay Burnett finds herself stranded in primitive, sultry West Africa. There, escaping from sinister German Kurt Mulheim, she encounters ivory trader Rick Morell — but Rick has vowed to distrust all women . . . How Gay endures the rigours of the slave market and escapes from her enemies to find true love is told in this torrid novel of the 'Gold Coast' in its pre-war days.

Books by Denise Robins
in the Ulverscroft Large Print Series:

THE FEAST IS FINISHED
I SHOULD HAVE KNOWN
A PROMISE IS FOR EVER
MORE THAN LOVE
THE SNOW MUST RETURN

DENISE ROBINS

SET THE STARS ALIGHT

Complete and Unabridged

ULVERSCROFT
Leicester

First published in Great Britain

First Large Print Edition
published August 1995

British Library CIP Data

Robins, Denise
    Set the stars alight.—Large print ed.—
Ulverscroft large print series: romance
I. Title
823.912 [F]

ISBN 0–7089–3352–1

Published by
F. A. Thorpe (Publishing) Ltd.
Anstey, Leicestershire
Set by Words & Graphics Ltd.
Anstey, Leicestershire
Printed and bound in Great Britain by
T. J. Press (Padstow) Ltd., Padstow, Cornwall

This book is printed on acid-free paper

Part One

Part One

Bom 07/02

1

IT was sweltering hot.

Gay Burnett lay on her narrow and none too comfortable bed under the mosquito netting of her bedroom, and gasped. She felt almost too hot, too languid, to fan herself. And she was wearing nothing but a thin cotton Japanese wrap. But oh, it was hot on the Gold Coast, and this cheap hotel was badly ventilated. She felt very tired, and when she closed her eyes she dreamed of an English spring and the cool dew and dusk.

No use to dream of that. She was thousands of miles from England and spring. She was one of a small film company brought out to West Africa by a German-American who was supposed to be making a wonder-film with one of the loneliest, hottest parts of Africa for its setting.

Of course, he was crazy. Gay realized that. The weather conditions were all against them, and they hadn't the capital to do things on the grand scale. All the members of the cast were complaining, and last night it had been rumoured that Mulheim, the manager, was 'broke'. Gay shuddered to think what would happen if that were really the case.

She reproached herself for being foolish enough to come to such an outlandish spot as Liberia with Kurt Mulheim's company. She was playing only a very small part because she had little experience, no particular talent, and only her beauty to recommend her — and her pay was small. But she had been so keen to get away from the dreary and fruitless search for work in London.

Her mind reverted to the years behind her, and her memories were not altogether happy ones, and did not cheer her up. Somehow she seemed always to have been alone. Her first remembrances were of a big house, an old greystone vicarage in the depths of the country where she was born. The Cotswold hills. Her grandfather had been Vicar there. Her mother, widowed in the first year of the Great War, had returned to her old home soon after

Jack Burnett found an untimely grave 'somewhere in France'. But when little Gay became aware of life, she was not the spoiled darling of grandfather and mother, the happy little girl that one might expect to find. Neither did the big ivy-clad house which stood on the crest of a hill, braving wind and rain in the long winter months, ring with her childish laughter.

The Reverend Theodore Lawton was a man of fanatical ideas, of harsh and unbending principles. He had disapproved of his daughter's marriage to her soldier, who, although a gentleman by birth and education, was a ranker, and had died as a 'Tommy'. Mr. Lawton, for all his religion, had been a snob. He had meant that his only child, Margaret, should marry well. He had refused to give her wedding his blessing, and to meet her husband, from the hour of their marriage. Only when Jack Burnett died a hero's death and received a Military Medal did the reverend gentleman relent, and consent to take his daughter back to the vicarage, and harbour her child when it was born.

But it was a severe and humourless atmosphere into which Gay was ushered. Gay! Ironic name for poor Margaret Burnett to have chosen for her fatherless babe. But she had wanted passionately for the little daughter to get the happiness, the joy out of life, that she, Margaret, had known only for a few short weeks with her Jack, and then lost again.

Alas, her ambitions for the baby Gay did not materialize! For when Gay was four years old Mrs. Burnett followed her husband to the grave. And one of the child's first recollections was being taken by her grandfather, the tall, austere, terrible old man, to the very graveside, and made to stand with him there and watch the earth being shovelled on to her mother's coffin. The child hardly understood what was happening. She only knew that she was terrified and lonely, and that when she screamed wildly and begged to be taken home her grandfather reprimanded her and preached her a sermon on the necessity to learn self-control early in life.

That grim funeral day, when the Cotswolds were white with snow and a bitter wind was blowing, was never to be forgotten by Margaret Burnett's luckless child. And the years that followed were as bitter, as unrelenting, as the sharp east wind. Loneliness was Gay's portion. Always alone, except for a succession of dreary nursemaids, none of whom stayed long, because they disliked the rigours of the cold, bare vicarage, where indoor every conceivable economy was practised, and outside the garden was overgrown and decayed. Little Gay was, therefore, flung to the mercy of servants, or those of the Vicar's parishioners who took pity on the little girl who had been orphaned at such a tender age.

When Gay was in her teens she was lovely to look at, with all the grace, the gold and white and pink beauty which had been her sole heritage from a lovely mother and a father who, in his university days, had been known as 'Beau Jack'. But it was a beauty which was little asset in the vicarage, where Gay was taught that beauty was a woman's curse, and that she must avoid temptation to pander to vanity; where all mirrors were discouraged and the money allowed her by her grandfather for clothing herself was almost negligible. Gay learned at an early age to buy a few yards of cheap material and run up her own dresses, and to knit and sew for herself.

But that state of affairs, almost Brontë-like in its grimness, its solitude, came to an end when Gay reached her twentieth birthday. The Reverend Mr. Lawton died, and his living and the vicarage passed with him.

Then Gay, a much-repressed creature, timid, lacking in self-confidence, utterly ignorant of life, was suddenly plunged into an altogether new era. A life in London, which, after her convent-like existence in the Cotswolds came to her as a staggering revelation.

She was offered a home by a second cousin of her father, one of the few relatives he had possessed. A widow who lived in a small house near Paddington Station and had at one time been on the stage. At forty she was still good-looking, and sometimes obtained small character parts in film studios.

From the moment that Gay was established in Gladys Burnett's house she was rid of all the repressions and inhibitions caused by that aimless and destructive existence which her old grandfather had forced her to lead. There was no more loneliness for Gay. No more pinching and scraping, although Cousin Gladys, as Gay called her, was far from well off. But she had small private means and a nature which encouraged her to spend twice as much as she possessed. She was the exact opposite of Theodore Lawton, and had he known her he would undoubtedly have condemned her to burn in the fires of hell. Gay was well aware of that. Yet Cousin Gladys was far from bad. She was a good creature, one of the most generous and kindly women Gay had ever met, and, for the short, dazzling year that Gay lived with her she was both the mother and father that Gay had always needed.

The little house was always filled with people, mostly young and of the theatrical and film world. Gay soon lost her shyness, became aware of the fact that she was beautiful and that men admired her, and aware also of the fact that she had the natural ability to sing and dance. She had

not been with Cousin Gladys a month
before she had received some strenuous
private coaching from that old trouper,
and was taken by her from one film
studio to another to get 'tests' and try
for 'walk-on' parts if she could not do
better.

It was a glorious year for Gay, on
the whole. *Life* after the death-in-life
existence in the vicarage. But it ended
all too soon. A chill seized Cousin
Gladys, and pneumonia followed. Death
once more left the girl alone in the world.
This time a much more experienced
Gay, and not the ignorant, terrified,
shrinking young creature whom Gladys
had first taken under her wing. But
still a Gay of complete innocence.
Among the many men whom she had
met in film studios and her cousin's
house, not one had attracted her to
anything more than ordinary friendship.
Love — the overwhelming, passionate
kind of emotion which had driven her
mother into the arms of a penniless
soldier twenty-one years ago — had not
yet come Gay's way.

The death of Gladys revealed a sea of

unpaid debts, and the sale by creditors of her home and its contents. And Gay was once more without funds, without work, and with all the difficulties to face which usually beset a pretty girl who has no family.

It was then — hanging round one of the lesser film studios — that she met Iris Power, who introduced her to the German-American Mulheim, who had formed this company and brought them all out to Liberia.

It had sounded an enticing proposition. The glamour of the East, and a certain job. Gay had no ties and was ready and willing enough to sail with the others who signed Mulheim's contract.

Well — here she was in Africa; with all the glamour she had wanted; sunshine, colour, natives; wonderful scenery. But the glamour faded somewhat when one was so hot, so badly fed and housed, and doubtful about the success of the company.

The bedroom door burst open. A tall, red-headed girl with a white, frightened face, burst into the room. She was wearing a blue cotton dress and a big

11

hat of coarse native straw. She flung the hat on the bed and rushed at Gay.

"Well — that's *done* it!" she said.

Gay sat up, startled.

"Iris — what's up?"

Iris Power, one of the 'walk-ons' on Mulheim's Company, made her way under the mosquito netting, sat on the bed and put her head between her hands.

"Mulheim has just been seeing the whole company," she said. "We're done — busted — stranded, kid. Isn't it a shame?"

Gay's heart gave a twist. She felt queer and sick. So it had happened. The rumour had not been without foundation. She stared blindly at Iris.

"Oh, lord — what's it mean?" she asked.

"A week's pay and dismissal. Mulheim says he's sorry, but the company's failed. All the work we've done out here this last four weeks is wasted. Rotten management, that's what I call it. And anyhow, I don't trust that German. He's nothing but a rotten German twister who calls himself a Yank, and we were fools to come out with him."

"But it's frightful, Iris!" said Gay. "We can't pay our own passages home again."

"I know that," said Iris bitterly. "And not only *that*." Mulheim says there's trouble brewing in Europe. Britain may be at war with Germany soon. I think that is what is getting old Kurt."

"What'll you do?"

"Well, Billy Freeland's got a bit of cash and he's crazy about me. He says if I like to marry him he'll take me to South Africa, to a place called Port Elizabeth, where he has pals, and see if we can get a job together there."

"Are you going?"

"Yes."

Gay's brain felt sticky; as though her thoughts could not flow. She got up and began to dress, slowly. Iris would go to Port Elizabeth with Billy Freeland — one of the 'supers' in the company, and the only one with private means. So Iris was all right. And the others, the bigger parts who got bigger pay, would be all right. But she — with a few pounds in her pocket — what in heaven's name could she do, stranded on the West Coast?

Stranded! An ugly, terrifying word.

"Mulheim was asking for you, kid," said Iris wearily; "better go down and see him and get your pay."

Gay finished dressing. She regarded her reflection in the small cracked mirror of the dressing table — bamboo, like the rest of the furniture — before she left. Even the heat, hard work and conditions of the last four weeks had not destroyed that radiant white-and-gold beauty that had induced Kurt Mulheim to give the English girl a part, despite her lack of serious film experience. In the thin white linen dress with a scarlet belt round her waist, she looked a child; slender, graceful, exquisite, with her pale skin and soft gold hair cut short and waving naturally back from her forehead. Her wide-set eyes, very blue and limpid and black-lashed, were curiously innocent. The eyes of a young, eager girl not yet disillusioned or cynical. That innocent, almost virginal appearance was Gay's chief charm. Men went crazy about her.

These few weeks in Liberia in Mulheim's film company had depressed her, but her

14

spirit was by no means daunted.

Everybody in the company had been nice to her — the 'kid' of the company. The only thing that worried Gay was that the German himself had been *too* nice. A few nights ago when they had met on the stairs in the hotel as she was going up to bed he had stopped her and told her that she looked like an angel, ascending heavenwards. He had touched her arm, given her a look, whispered a word which even she could not fail to understand. Innocent she might be, but by no means ignorant about life and men, after her travels with this somewhat rough company. She had bidden Mulheim good night haughtily; but she had not escaped him before he had said:

"One day I am going to make you kiss me good night, you Golden Girl . . . *meine Liebchen.*"

She detested him; the rather plump blond man with his straw-coloured hair, his red lips and his too-perfect clothes, his light-coloured eyes behind the thick lenses of his powerful glasses. He might be a good film-producer, but he was a hateful personality. There was something brutal about him which all the girls feared. Well, now he had failed with the company — he was still more contemptible.

Gay's interview with Kurt Mulheim took place on the verandah of the hotel. She sat in a basket chair beside him and drank the iced orange which he had ordered her and smoked a cigarette with him because he insisted. But she hated the way he looked at her. She kept her gaze on the scene before her. The strange motley crowd — mostly natives — passing up and down the streets in front of the hotel which overlooked a bazaar. Here were rich-coloured rugs for sale; here bizarre jugs and bowls and silver or brass ornaments. Bright-coloured parrots and humming-birds perched in golden cages; stalls bearing ripe fruits; coconuts, persimmons, pineapples, custard-apples and passion fruit. The air was harsh with the sound of chattering native voices, the screech of the parrots, the faint boom of gongs.

Glamour and romance enough; but Gay felt afraid and bitterly homesick for England as she looked upon the brilliant scene and watched the dark motley crowd passing before her. This was a town where English and Americans were to be found. But it was on the fringe of a desert peopled with lawless, savage tribes. She was afraid to be left alone, stranded in this place. And Mulheim was only repeating what Iris had told her, apologizing for the failure . . . but there is was, he said . . . there were no funds left . . . things had not gone right. The company must break up and disperse.

"But there is no need for such fear to come into those beautiful blue eyes of yours," Mulheim finished softly, and bent nearer her, his short-sighted eyes beaming through the spectacles.

Gay drew back from him. He was repellent, this too-fat man who claimed American citizenship and was so definitely a German. She looked at the plump white fingers that held the meerschaum pipe he was smoking, and shivered to think of them touching her.

"If you would tell me, please, Mr. Mulheim," she said, "how to get a passage back to England . . . how to get enough money . . . "

"Ah! Now you must listen to my plans," he said. "We have failed, and my syndicate cannot go on supplying money for our film out here. But I have a nest-egg of my own, and if you will be nice to me, *kleine* Gay . . . "

She stood up at once. She might have known this was coming.

"I'm sorry," she said coldly. "but I think this sort of talk is a waste of time."

He was on his feet instantly, and swiftly put out a hand to detain her.

"Don't be silly, little one. Listen to me. You have said you want to go back to England. Very well. I will take you back — if you will come — as my wife. There I will marry you. You shall go to New York as my wife. Perhaps also to Berlin."

Her cheeks coloured hotly, but she shook her head.

"Thank you, but I — can't possibly accept your kind offer."

"Why not?"

"I don't love you," she said simply.

His eyes seemed to recede to pin-points, peering at her . . . feasting on her fragile loveliness. Kurt Mulheim was mad to have this young girl, even at the price of marriage. She was the woman he had always wanted; very young and pure, and with her pale gold hair and blue, wide eyes, so like the blonde women of Germany. The promise of passion in the curve of her lips and that pale, slender throat, where he could see the scared pulse beating, drew him out of his usual shell. Kurt Mulheim had never before contemplated marriage.

"I adore you," he said with sudden passion. *"Ich liebe dich.* Marry me tomorrow — and we will travel together and I will spend every pound I have saved — on you. We will visit my home in New York and later I am returning to Germany. I have land there — more money — you shall be a queen. You shall become a loyal servant of my Fuehrer. That is what I am, Gay. I am no American, except when it suits me to work there for my Fatherland."

"No — stop — please! I'm sorry — I can't marry you," she broke in. "Mr. Mulheim — "

"No, no — you must call me Kurt . . . "

Her delicate brows drew together.

"Mr. Mulheim — you must take 'no' for an answer."

His thick fleshy nostrils flared slightly. For an instant Gay thought he was going to storm at her. His plump face grew livid. Kurt Mulheim did not like being rejected by a slip of a girl whom he had honoured with a proposal. Then a queer look came into his eyes. He drew back from her and bowed, his topee in his hand.

"As you will — for the moment. But Kurt Mulheim does not take 'no' for an answer — as you shall see."

He turned and left her. Gay stood a moment looking blindly out at the glittering pageant of the native bazaar. She was growing more frightened every moment. To be left here in this hotel . . . with that man pursuing her . . . it was awful. She must get away . . . away from West Africa . . . to England.

The question was how to do it. She had a little less than eight pounds in her possession. Not nearly enough to take her to Port Elizabeth, where Iris was going. She might appeal to some of the others in the company, but no doubt they were all hard up and hard put to it — sacked at a week's notice. She was too proud to beg. No — if she had to fight, then she must fight alone. Gay did not lack courage. It was that hard, indomitable streak in her which was the legacy of old Theodore Lawton to his grand-daughter. The Lawtons never gave in. Gay would not give in.

But what could she do?

A tall, bronzed man in khaki-coloured shorts and wearing a topee came up the steps of the hotel and bumped into Gay. Immediately he stepped back and apologized, sweeping off the topee with almost ironic courtesy.

"I *beg* your pardon!"

His voice was low, deep, drawling a little. Gay looked at him. An Englishman; a very handsome one, with striking eyes, curiously light grey in the dark, sun-browned face; thick brown hair, a powerful nose and chin; a well-shaped mouth, though it was the weakest feature in an otherwise strong face.

An attractive man — so tall that Gay had to look up to him. But disappointing

21

because she could not fail to see that he had quite definitely been drinking. Flushed cheeks, unsteady gait, foolish smile revealed that fact. Then he admitted the fact openly.

"I'm blind," he said, with a beatific smile. "Quite blind. Must be — otherwise wouldn't have knocked into a pretty girl like that. Mos' ungentlemanny . . . do forgive me."

He put on his topee again, rocking a little on his feet. Gay looked at the bronzed and inebriated young man and, without a word, turned her back on him.

He at once followed her and caught her arm.

"Don't run away — haven't said you forgive me. Do come and talk to me, Blue Eyes. I *hate* women with blue eyes. Don't trust 'em — but they're damned fascinating — " He broke off with a laugh.

Gay dragged her arm away, scarlet, furious.

"How dare you!"

He blinked at her. Then the topee came off again. He grew very solemn.

"I *beg* your pardon. You're an angel. Ought to have known. But most blue-eyed women are devils. So long, sweetheart."

He walked away, still very solemn, and vanished into the bar. Gay, puzzled, stared after him. What a curious man; with a strange personality. If he lacked sobriety, he certainly did not lack charm. She half wished that he had been sober and that she could have talked to him. Something about the young man had appealed to her curiosity.

Then she forgot about him and went up to her room.

2

IRIS POWER had packed and left the hotel with Billy Freeland. She was going to marry him — a man she did not love — for the sake of a protector and financial security.

All the rest of the company had gone, too. Drifted away. Where, Gay did not know. She only knew that she, personally, had no plans, no idea what to do, and that she was alone. But she also knew that her former employer was still there, a menace in the background, worrying her.

Iris had called her stupid not to accept Mulheim's proposal of marriage.

"He's not bad-looking in a Teutonic fashion and he's quite clever and interesting, and if he has private means — I'd do it," Iris had said.

Yes, Iris would have done it. She was built that way. But Gay could not. She was otherwise constructed. To her, it would be like selling one's body to a man . . . to marry him just for money.

Besides, Mulheim did not even interest her as a friend. She did not trust him. She was afraid of him. It was inherent in her to hate Germans. Germany had killed her young father, twenty-two years ago. She could never forget that. She decided to go to the British Consulate in the morning and ask for advice and help, rather than appeal to anybody in this horrible hotel.

It had been late afternoon when Mulheim had dismissed his company . . . too late for Gay to see the British Consul or take any steps to get away from the town by herself.

When the sun went down and it was cooler Gay strolled into the garden at the back of the hotel. The giant palms and date trees were black against a pale sky that blazed with stars. A wonderful warm night. A night for romance; with the throb of native drums in the air . . . drum-messages, sent hundred of miles across Africa from camp to camp.

But Gay was lonely and afraid, and would have given much to wake up and find herself in London in Cousin Gladys's snug little house, instead of in this exotic moonlit garden, or even the desolate lonely vicarage in the Cotswolds where she had had such a wretched childhood.

The fragrance of a Turkish cigarette was suddenly wafted to her . . . and she came upon the white-clad figure of a man also taking a solitary stroll in the hotel grounds. He was bare-headed. She at once recognized him as the man who had bumped into her on the verandah this afternoon.

He seemed quite sober now. He smiled in recognition as he came face to face with her.

"If it isn't the golden angel I annoyed a few hours ago!" he said. "Well, Blue Eyes, you look like an alabaster statue in the moonlight. What are you doing, wandering alone under the African stars? Aren't you afraid somebody will carry you off?"

Gay — against her own will — was attracted by the man, although angry at his brazen conduct. She tried not to smile. She said:

"Look here — I don't know you, and — "

"Oh, everybody out here knows me," he broke in. "My name's Rick Morrell, otherwise Richard. But you can call me Rick. I'm a trader . . . I trade in ivories on the coast — make a lot of money and spend most of it in getting tight. Shocking, isn't it?"

"Yes," said Gay, "it *is* shocking."

His eyes, handsome, sardonic, suddenly widened. He pitched away his cigarette.

"I do believe you really are horrified."

"Naturally I am," she said coldly.

He flung back his handsome head and laughed. Gay crimson, started to walk away, but he called her back.

"Don't run away. I've never met a girl out here whom I can really shock. Most women shock me!"

"If you think I find you amusing, you are wrong," said Gay. "I think you're contemptible and rather impertinent."

He became serious.

"Do you really, Blue Eyes? I'd like to talk to you, you know, and I don't mean to offend you. English girls are rare out here, and you're rather like an English rose. Don't run away too soon. Give me a moment's grace."

Gay stood still. His voice was haunting, and quite gentle now, and his eyes queer, lonely. She knew that loneliness. She was distressed to find her own eyes filling with tears. She herself was utterly alone and afraid of Africa. She needed a friend, badly.

The Englishman, Rick Morrell, drew nearer her.

"What's the matter, little thing?" he asked abruptly. "Is anything wrong. Are you by yourself in this goddamned place?"

"Yes, I'm up against it," she blurted out.

"*Really* up against it?"

"Yes. Stranded here . . . with only eight pounds in the world . . . and I don't know where to go or what to do."

Rick Morrell looked intently down at the pale little face. How lovely it was. How pure in the moonlight, he thought. The glitter of tears on her long lashes stirred him. He told himself he was a damn' fool to be moved by a woman's tears. After the way Lydia had treated him, he'd vowed never to let a woman's weeping touch his heart again.

Lydia had had blue eyes like this girl . . . Lydia had been young and divinely fair and graceful. And she had let him down, given him a raw, rotten deal. And, God, how she had lied! Hadn't he vowed never to believe another word a woman said?

But on an impulse Gay, sorely in need of help from one of her countrymen, began to pour out her story. Rick Morrell heard all about the failure of the film company; the sudden dismissal with a week's salary; and Kurt Mulheim, the manager, who called himself 'American' and who was pursuing her.

"He follows me everywhere. I always see him in the background. I'm terrified of him," finished Gay. "What am I to do? Where am I to go? Tell me what you think . . . "

Rick Morrell was drawn to her, moved despite all his inner convictions that women were liars and traitors. This girl, Gay Burnett, looked a mere child.

"Something ought to be done about you," he said. "Something *must* be done. You can't be left high and dry in a place like this. It's unthinkable."

"I thought of going to the British Consul."

"The wisest thing to do," said Rick.

Silence a moment. Then with a shy, sad smile that haunted the man long afterwards, Gay held out her hand.

"It's late. I must go in. Good night."

He stared at the small white hand. Then he said tersely:

"Good night . . . But I'm not fit to take that little hand, my dear."

"That can't be true," said Gay. "You've been so kind. Don't be silly, Rick. Shake hands."

"But you saw what I was like . . . when we first met."

"You aren't often like that — are you? And anyhow, there's no reason why we shouldn't shake hands and be friends."

"I'm no fit friend for any decent girl." He gave a sardonic laugh. The whole of his personality seemed to change. He had been so nice, so interested in her just now, but suddenly she saw him again as a different being; a man with the devil in his heart, with hell in his eyes. "Always tight. Pleasant, isn't it? But drink's the only anodyne . . . the only relief from pain . . . from memory. I don't want to be sober, to have to think . . . to talk to women like you . . . and remember *her*."

Gay's heart beat fast. She was half afraid of the strange Englishman in this mood, yet still attracted by him against her will.

"Who is it you want to forget?" she asked curiously.

"A girl with eyes like yours — a little liar and a traitor!" he said harshly. And added: "Good night."

"Oh, where are you going?" she asked without knowing why she asked it.

"To the bar for a few more drinks," she heard the reply and the ironic laugh following it as he disappeared behind the palm trees.

Gay stared after him. She thought:

"What a pity — what a tragedy — a splendid man like that — wrecking himself with drink because of a woman. A man that any woman might have adored . . . "

Yes, it was queer she should feel like that about him; that she bothered to hate the thought of him soaking . . . in the bar . . .

A touch of her shoulder startled her. She gave a little scream and swung round.

"Oh, *you!*"

It was Kurt Mulheim, suave, smiling, perfectly dressed as ever in his immaculate white suit. His close-cropped fair head was shining in the moonlight. An ugly square head. A square Germanic face. Instinctively the girl recoiled from him.

"All alone?" he greeted her.

"I'm just going in," she said. "Good night."

"No — surely not yet," he said quietly. "You have had time to talk for half an hour to that drunken sot of an Englishman."

Gay drew in her breath.

"You were spying on me — were you?"

For an instant Kurt Mulheim looked as though he were going to have an apoplectic fit. Face and bull-neck turned brick red and his eyes suffused behind the glasses. His hand clenched.

He did not like that word 'spy'. But he had himself under control in a few minutes. Intuitively his hand went to his breast pocket. He patted it gently while his face cleared and he eyed the girl almost benevolently. He knew perfectly well that the remark had come by pure chance from her innocent lips. She could have no possible idea that he was out here in Africa solely in the interests of his Fuehrer. That he had lived in America, posing as an American citizen for the last two years, under the control of an organized band of Nazi agents, spreading their propaganda through the United States. Propaganda was needed out here too. The Germans wanted colonies. In Africa they used to have many. But England had removed them. Kurt Mulheim loathed England with all the strength of his German soul. But he did not loathe this young and lovely English girl who had come out with the film company. Of course, he had known all along that the company would fail, but that did not matter. Before disbanding it, he had secured for Germany the services of two of his troupe — a young dancer, a Hungarian girl, and a violinist from Italy. They had not been turned adrift quite like the others. They had good

German money in their pocket and they had promised to send him certain information which he required, from the big cities like Johannesburg and Cape Town where they would next be employed.

Gay Burnett seemed to Mulheim not so much fair game as a valuable ally. As his wife, once she became a German citizen, she would be such an admirable dupe. She would mix with and talk to Englishmen of importance to whom Kurt would see that she had an introduction. She would look like a little nun. She would fox them all with that demure, baby face of hers, and they would think her loyal to her former country. But once she was Frau Mulheim she would serve the Fuehrer. About that Kurt had made up his mind. And if love and admiration did not draw her into matrimony with him, he would use more forcible methods.

Gay said:

"I hate people who eavesdrop . . . "

Then Mulheim spoke with perfect equanimity:

"Spying is an ugly word. But it is

34

natural a man should guard jealously the girl he is going to marry."

"You are mad," said Gay; "I'm not going to marry you."

Mulheim's eyes narrowed to slits. His thick lower lip protruded.

"Come, Golden Girl — you had a few smiles and soft glances for that inebriated Englishman. I saw them. Can you not spare a few for Kurt?"

"No. The other man is my countryman. Anyhow, I don't like Germans."

Mulheim's eyes flickered dangerously. When he had this proud contemptuous young girl in his possession he would punish her for that. But he smiled.

"Once you are my wife — you take *my* nationality — American."

"German, you mean."

"German if you prefer it. I thought you did not."

Her temper flared up. She stamped her foot.

"Get it into your head that I won't marry you."

"Did you expect Mr. Morrell to offer you a home?" Mulheim suddenly asked her.

"What do you know of Mr. Morrell, anyhow?"

"Everybody out here knows . . . his name is a byword in the drinking saloons."

Without knowing why, Gay found herself protecting the Englishman.

"If he drinks too much — so do most men out here."

"He is sodden with it," said Mulheim. "Well on the road to ruin. For love of a woman. It is a common story. Poor weak fool! I have met and talked with traders out here who shrug their shoulders about him. He was doing excellently until he met this woman, an English lady, Lydia Brett. She made him crazy about her, with her red-gold hair and her white skin. She became engaged to him and threw him over the day before their wedding for an old man with a fortune."

Gay was silent a moment. She thought, painfully, of the handsome, attractive Englishman, drinking himself to death . . . to find solace from pain because he had loved, trusted and been jilted for so contemptible a reason. An old man with money. Morrell must have loved Lydia

36

a very great deal, she reflected, for the tragedy to have affected him so vitally.

"He is a spineless fool," came Mulheim's guttural voice. "There are other women in the world — as beautiful and as fair and desirable — like you — my future wife . . . "

"Don't be so ridiculous . . . " began Gay.

But suddenly he caught her in his arms in a passionate embrace. He kissed her crazily, his fingers catching at the pale gold of her hair.

"Mine, *mein Liebchen* . . . and you *are* going to be mine!" he said violently.

For an instant Gay felt nothing but anger and disgust in that close embrace. Her heart was sick within her at the thought of all that this signified. For this man had brought her out here — thousands of miles from England. She was afraid of being alone here in this African hotel with a man like Kurt Mulheim. He was a cunning, dangerous man, and in her heart she believed him to be a German spy. She knew that there was nobody on earth to help her escape from him tonight. Tomorrow she could go to the Consul. *But tomorrow might be too late.* "Come, come, kiss me and don't be a little fool," came Mulheim's voice. And suddenly, in an extremity of fear, Gay screamed aloud . . . and she screamed the name of the one and only Englishman whom she knew in this forsaken place.

"Rick Morrell! Oh, Rick Morrell!" The shrill, terror-laden young voice rang through the quiet night; piercing the smoke-laden atmosphere of the hotel bar, where men of all nationalities stood drinking, smoking, talking.

Rick Morrell was propped against the bar, a gin-and-lime in his hand. It was a fine, sensitive hand, but not very steady. He was half drunk, but he heard that terrified voice from the garden.

"Rick Morell! Oh, Rick Morrell!" He crashed his glass down on the counter and stared out of the open window at the moon-drenched garden, his eyes a bit bemused.

"In God's name, what's that?" he muttered. "A woman calling me. It's that girl . . . that little English girl who had Lydia's eyes . . . "

The next moment he was outside; no longer stupefied with drink, but clear-headed, and quite sober. It did not take him long to reach that part of the garden beyond the palm trees where he had said good night to Gay Burnett. And when he saw the small slender figure in white struggling in the arms of a man whom he recognized as the film producer who was nothing more or less than a German Nazi agent, he went blind with rage.

However much he distrusted women, Rick was not going to stand by and see a girl treated like that by a swine of a foreigner.

Rick's lean clenched fist smashed into Mulheim's plump face, and sent him reeling back from Gay. He crashed into a palm and slithered on to the ground. Rick knew how to box. At Oxford (that seemed to him in the dim ages past, although less than ten years ago), as a boy of twenty-one, he had won the heavy-weight championship. Mulheim hadn't a chance. His smug blond looks would be marred for many a day. He lay there without making a sound, the blood trickling from his chin.

"He's taken the count," said Rick solemnly, then laughed as he looked at the girl. "Are you all right?"

"Yes," she whispered. But she was shaking and in tears. The encounter with Mulheim had been singularly unpleasant and she felt her lips had been smirched by his kisses.

"Do you know the gentleman now unconscious?" asked Rick Morrell, lighting a cigarette. His fuddled brain had cleared completely.

"My — my manager. At least he was," said Gay and blew her small nose forlornly. "Don't you remember? I told you I was so . . . afraid of Kurt Mulheim."

"H'm," said Rick. "Well, he'll stay asleep for a few minutes, anyhow, if you want to get away."

Mulheim was half-conscious now. He groaned. Gay suddenly appealed to Morrell. He might be a drunken fool, but at least he had saved her, had championed her cause grandly. She said:

"Oh, please, please, don't leave me here alone! I'm frightened to death of what that beast might do when he comes round. Later, perhaps, when I'm in my room — there are no locks on the doors — " She gulped and paused, her cheeks crimson, her eyes full of tears.

Rick Morrell stared down into those very blue eyes for an instant, without speaking. God, how like Lydia she was, he thought, and no doubt at heart she was just as fickle, as unreliable, as mercenary. Lydia had sold herself to an old man. To old Roger Milcroft, an American millionaire who had wanted her youth and fair beauty and had bought them over the head of love, with his unlimited supply of dollars.

The months seemed to roll back, and Rick Morrell was no longer here in the moon-drenched African garden. He was in England. In London on a certain warm June night at a private dance given by one of Mayfair's well-known society hostesses.

Lydia had been at that dance. It was the first time he had met her. Nobody seemed to know much about her. The hostess had come across her in a party in Monte Carlo that previous winter. She was in the early twenties, without family . . . she had given out to the world that she had lost both father and mother in a fatal air accident . . . and she was companion to an American widow who lived most of her time in the South of France. Rick's hostess had been captivated like everybody else by Lydia's extraordinary beauty and a quality of almost diamond brightness which clung to her; a most engaging amiability. She loved everybody and they loved her. She had a laugh like the note of a flute and a peculiarly high child-like voice. (Rick winced at the mere memory of that crystal-clear voice. He had thought that it must belong to a soul as sweet and as crystalline as her voice. But he had been mistaken.) Perhaps he was not altogether to blame. Everyone had been mistaken in Lydia. She had duped them all. Only when they came to know her better did her newly acquired friends and associates get below the surface and find a scheming little adventuress. A creature without heart or soul. A gold-digger without sense of shame and with the natural ability to use her ethereal appearance and her baby voice in order to entrap the unsuspecting victim in her toils.

Later Rick had learned, too, that Lydia had neither good birth nor breeding behind her, but was the child of an English father and a German mother of doubtful origin. She had escaped from them at an early age, and found a benefactor to give her a good education. Later, on account of her amazing beauty and personal magnetism, and with a knowledge of languages, she had worked her way on a tissue of plausible stories into society. Whereby she had met the American widow, who gave her a job, and later Rick Morrell, who offered her his hand and his heart.

Always he remembered his first glimpse of Lydia in that Mayfair mansion. She had burst upon his sight like a radiant vision from another world. He, at the time, was living with a widowed mother, working desperately hard as a civil engineer, and more interested in his work than in women. But Lydia walked straight through that wall of indifference, into his very heart. A small, slender girl with fragile bones . . . just like this girl,

Gay Burnett . . . tiny, yet perfect. The 'pocket Venus'! Only Lydia's hair was flaming red . . . full of gold lights, and curling crisply down to her slender neck. Lydia's skin was as pale and creamy as milk, and her eyes (like Gay's) large, blue, with heavy lids on which there were fascinating bluish shadows. On that particular night when Rick Morrell saw her first she wore a white Victorian ballgown of billowing chiffon, sewn with tiny flowers, and a low corsage of flowers from which her dimpled shoulders and swan-neck emerged as beautiful and pure as alabaster.

The hostess had said:

"Rick, you must meet Lydia. Until you have danced with her, you have never danced at all. So all my men tonight are telling me."

Lydia had placed a tiny hand in his . . . so small, so fragile and ringless. He had clasped it gently, almost afraid to hurt her, and thought it the hand of a child, as gentle as her smile. Now he knew that small hand was open wide for all that the world could place into it, and that those delicate fingers would

44

not hesitate to take the heart of any man and break it in pieces if it suited her to do so.

She had given him that sublime smile which he so well recalled, and said:

"Don't let's dance. One can always dance. But I'd rather talk to *you*."

Flattery. Lydia did everything by flattery and persuasion. He had thought it grand to be singled out by her for conversation. So they had both talked and danced, and when he first waltzed with her to an old Viennese tune she was light as thistledown in his arms — he had fallen desperately and feverishly in love with her. The first acute love of Rick Morrell's life. A love which burnt him up and swamped his very existence while it lasted. A love which he now knew to be a wild passion belying the more noble name.

Rick had never done anything by halves. When he worked he gave his whole time to it. He found that loving Lydia was also a whole-time job. Without appearing so to do, she sapped his time, his vitality and what money he possessed. She was a person who wanted all or nothing. So he gave all. Spent every penny he had saved since his Oxford days. Spent more than he could afford. Bought her lovely, extravagant presents. Went without things he needed, in order to keep her supplied daily with expensive flowers. Sold his most valued possessions in order that the ring he bought for her should be a diamond worthy of her bewildering beauty.

This in June. In August Lydia announced that her American employer had returned to New York. Her explanation was that the woman was recalled urgently on business. Amongst other things that Rick afterwards heard, he discovered that Lydia had attracted a man whom the elder woman wanted for herself, and in a fit of jealousy and pique the American had dismissed her too-charming companion. Lydia now appealed to Rick. He must leave his job, she said, leave England and his mother, go with her, Lydia, to Hollywood. She had been offered a marvellous job on the films. But she was madly in love with her Rick, she said, and could not go without him. He protested that if he left his job, he left his life's work and interest. Also he could not be dependent on his wife. He was not that sort of fellow. But Lydia was not to be done out of her 'playmate'. He was altogether too attractive as a lover. The best-looking, most amusing, most vital male being who had ever laid his heart at her feet. She was as near to really loving Rick as she had ever come in her calculating adventuresome young life. She cajoled, pleaded and wept. She even got a Hollywood producer to promise Rick an engineering job in Los Angeles if he would only go out there.

Rick gave in. Weak of him, and he knew it, but he loved his Lydia too much to leave her. And he was not going to watch her sail for California and know that that tiny, glittering figure crowned with flame-gold hair would be unprotected, open to any male creature's advances. Jealousy stormed at him. He ignored his mother's silent appeal. He flung up his job. His mother had a pension of her own. He sold out his remaining stocks and shares on the English market. He prepared to leave London, and he and Lydia were to be married the day before they boarded the *Queen Mary* for New York.

Even the honeymoon suite was engaged at a fabulous cost for Lydia. Almost Rick's last penny went on that. He kept just enough to see him through in Hollywood until he secured the job which Lydia's friend offered him.

One person alone knew that Rick was heading for disaster. The mother who adored him and who had been everything to him before Lydia came on the scene. The mother who had planned big things for her boy. Her handsome, clever Richard, who was all in all to her. For his sake Mrs. Morrell had accepted his engagement to Lydia. Everybody told her how lucky Rick was to find such a clever, amusing, lovely little creature. But Mrs. Morrell knew in her heart that Lydia was worthless. That she was sapping Rick of everything . . . even his moral strength. Rick had not been the same since he fell in love with Lydia. He was like one obsessed. His passion for her consumed him day and night. He had grown thin and haggard and harassed. He said that he was the happiest man in the world, but Mrs. Morrell wondered . . .

Two days before his wedding, Fate struck two bitter and mortal blows at Rick Morrell. His mother collapsed and died instantly, of angina. He had loved her, and it was a great loss, and an unexpected one. He had not even guessed that she had heart-trouble. She had kept it from him, just as she had kept most of her anxieties concerning Lydia. Naturally, it was to Lydia he turned for sympathy, for comfort. But when he went to find her, Lydia was missing. When he called at the hotel in which she was staying, and enquired for her, he found only a note. A poor attempt at apology; perhaps a genuine expression of regret. Lydia had walked out on him at the last moment. Her explanation was — money. She had always needed a lot of money. Of course, Rick had known that, much as he worshipped her. She had been afraid to go to Hollywood and risk finding that she was a failure on the screen. And afraid to tie herself to a penniless man without a job. (She forgot that it was she who had removed Rick's pennies and Rick's job.)

She had run away with an old man, an American. Roger Milcroft, the Chicago tinned-food millionaire. It was with him, as his wife, she intented to sail on the morrow, and not with Rick.

The young man staggered under the two successive blows. They were knock-outs. He could not now look back on the awful agony of his disillusionment, his sense of complete loss and failure when he walked away from Lydia's hotel, without feeling physically ill. It was an agony that left a mark on his soul, never to be erased.

The next twenty-four hours were hazy to him. He remembered walking all night through the street; pitching the little platinum wedding-ring which he had bought for Lydia into the river, cursing her and all women as it splashed and sank. He remembered returning to his home where his mother's body lay, and burning Lydia's photograph and all the little amorous notes she had ever written him, and a chiffon handkerchief to which there clung still a faint odour of her familiar French perfume. And later, finding a beggar in the streets, and pressing into his dirty hand a gold pencil which she had given him, and a silver lighter.

"Take them . . . sell them," he had said to the astonished 'down-and-out'. "They'll bring you a few shillings. To me they're just trash . . . "

Then the next day, the day the *Queen Mary* sailed without him, the bitter day of his mother's funeral, and after he had got rid of would-be kind friends and sympathizers . . . hating their sympathy, knowing they must think him a poor fool who had asked for trouble and got it . . . he reviewed his situation.

He found himself a ruined man. His old job had been filled. His bank balance was so small that he could not hope to start any kind of lucrative business. The eager, enthusiastic, hard-working young man, who had first been introduced to Lydia, was a financial and spiritual wreck.

He could not stand up to it. It had been too crushing a defeat. For he had trusted Lydia and believed in her as he believed in God. To find her a worthless, faithless, utterly despicable character was more than he could bear.

He began to drink . . .

He drank persistently, adding further ruin to nerves and health. He could not bear London . . . any of the places which reminded him of Lydia and that fatal companionship. He wanted to get away from their mutual associates, from the least memory of the love which her mercenary action had so degraded. And it was with alcohol that he had tried to burn up the memories which returned whenever he saw a slender girl with red hair, or with tiny hands and feet, or tinkling laugh like Lydia's.

He hated her so deeply now that he wished he had gone on to the *Queen Mary*, found Lydia in that honeymoon suite with her elderly Chicago sugar-daddy, and choked the life out of her. Stopped her from laughing . . . for ever.

Then he met a man who was at Oxford with him and who had liked Rick. He saw that the once fine and lovable boy was going steadily downhill. The man was going out to the Gold Coast to trade in ivories. He took Rick with him. For the last twelve months now Rick

52

had been working for him. He was still drinking, but he knew his job and he sobered up at times and did what was required of him. Some four or five weeks ago Ricks' friend died of fever. Rick was left to carry on the job. And now that he was here in Liberia he meant to stay. Wasn't it called 'the white man's grave'? Well, let it be his, he told himself. He never wished to return to England. Here he would remain, and go on leading his ruined life — trading in ivories — until death claimed him. If ever the nostalgia for his own country seized him, and if ever he suffered from regrets for lost opportunities and the clean sweet life of happier days in England, he stifled it. A man in his position, and with his past must have no regrets. They did not pay.

And now he found himself face to face with a girl who was so painfully reminiscent of Lydia that it was partly intolerable and partly a fascination. Gay Burnett was Lydia's height, and Gay had Lydia's big, limpid, long-lashed eyes, and that rather child-like dulcet voice. The only difference which his blurred gaze noticed was the hair. For Gay's was not fiery red, but pale as wheat with the sun rippling through it. And her lips were not so curved, so archaic, so sensuous. They were sweet and a little thin and repressed, as though she had suffered. Lydia had never suffered. But others, like himself, no doubt, she had thrust into hell.

He did not know whether to be violently uncivil and rough to Gay Burnett, or kind. He chose the latter course. For there were tears on her lashes — tears of genuine grief and fright — and all the old tenderness and chivalry in Rick Morrell had not died. It revived tonight. Poor little small thing, he thought. Africa — this cruel, hot, fever-ridden Gold Coast — was no place for a lonely English girl. And he could not tolerate the thought of her in that fat German's arms. He loathed the Germans he met trading out here. Bullies, braggarts, most of them.

He cast a scornful look at Mulheim's recumbent form.

"This is what one might call starting a private war," he said. "But there may be another bigger one soon . . . between the likes of that large malignant creature and myself."

"What do you mean?" Gay asked fearfully.

"Don't you read your papers, my child?"

"I . . . haven't read them lately."

"I always read them, drunk or sober. I listen to radios. I like to know what is taking place in the big, big world."

He laughed and lit a fresh cigarette from the end of the old.

Gay said:

"Tell me . . . what is happening?"

"Likelihood of war."

"War between whom?"

Rick prodded the German's form gently with his toe.

"His Nazi-ridden Government and ours."

"No, no, not another!"

"Yes, my child, another and much worse than the old."

"My father was killed on the Somme."

"Mine also. An old soldier. He fought in the Boer War too . . . " He looked down at her with fresh interest. "A link," he added bitterly. "A blood-link. Two helpless beings rendered fatherless, when their male parents were offered up as sacrifices for their country."

She was glad to know that he felt there was a link between them of any kind. She was so lonely and so afraid of that other man on the ground.

Rick said:

"The Munich Peace won't last. What Chamberlain did for us last summer can't last. This is July. Take it from me . . . in a month's time we shall be at war with the Germans . . . purging the world of Nazism. And about time too. I've met some of 'em out here. I believe your so-called film-producer to be one of their agents."

She drew a deep breath, too bewildered, too miserable to answer. She thought how well Rick Morrell could speak when he wished to. What a lot he knew, and how deeply he thought . . . when he allowed himself to do so. Why, why had he to go downhill just because of a woman?

"Oh, Rick," she said wretchedly, "what shall I do?"

"Join up as a Red Cross nurse, my dear, and I'll get into battle-dress and follow in my father's footsteps and die a glorious death for England."

She winced because he spoke so bitterly.

"You would do that if there were a war, wouldn't you?"

"Certainly . . . " A ghost of a smile lit up the ruined beauty of Rick's face. "Wouldn't you?"

"Yes. But when I asked you what I was to do, I didn't mean about war . . . I meant about *now*."

He glanced at Mulheim. The German was struggling into a sitting position.

"Come with me," Rick said suddenly, taking Gay's arm. "You'd better not stay in this damned hotel with this damned Nazi hanging about. Perhaps, my dear, he is a member of the Gestapo. Perhaps we shall both find ourselves in concentration camps. Have you Jewish blood in you? I trust not, for your sake. I have a remote trace of it . . . it would be bad for me . . . "

He laughed aloud. But Gay shivered and hurried him away.

"Don't," she said under her breath. "Don't anger Mr. Mulheim."

"I'm not afraid of Herr Mulheim. I'm afraid of nothing but pretty women," said Rick Morrell.

She bit her lip, walking with him quickly through the purple-shadowed gardens towards the hotel.

"I am packed and ready. Where can I go?"

"I have a bungalow. You can stay there. You'll be safe. I have a house-boy who would slit the throat of anyone most cheerfully on my behalf if he knew I wished it. He carries me home when I am too drunk to get there myself. He is a mother to me, the black son-of-a-gun."

"Oh, don't!" she protested. "Why do you belittle yourself? Why do you boast of . . . of always being tight?"

"One boasts of the things at which one shines. I am able to put down more alcohol than any other English trader on the Gold Coast, and still stand on my feet."

"It will kill you if you go on like this."

"That would be most kindly of it."

"Oh, don't!" she said again, as though the man's intense bitterness and indifference to life hurt her. There was so much to like in him. Yes, instinctively she liked Rick Morrell.

"Will you trust yourself in my bungalow, my little one?" he asked her.

"Yes," she said gravely.

"Brave of you."

"No. Didn't you say that you loathe women? It is you who shall be afraid of me tonight . . . not I of you."

He stared at her small serious face, which was cameo-pale in the moonlight, then burst out laughing.

"'Pon my soul, you amuse me, Gay. Isn't that your name? Well, Gay we'll be merry together, and neither shall be afraid of the other. Come along. I've got a ramshackle car, but it goes. Get your luggage and I'll be outside the hotel, waiting for you."

"I'm deeply grateful to you," she said.

He watched her flit into the hotel and strolled back to the bar to collect his hat. He grinned sardonically as he went.

"I'm crazy," he thought. "Crazy to believe in her. No doubt she is a second

Lydia and the rest — out for what she can get. God knows why I'm bothering about her. But I just feel I can't leave her here with all these blacks and that slug-like German around."

3

TEN o'clock that same night.

Gay, very tried and bewildered and anxious about her future, sat in the living-room of Rick Morrell's bungalow — a small, sparsely furnished place. Everything was dilapidated; the white curtains ragged, rotted by the wicked climate. A lamp with a torn parchment shade on a table bearing old newspapers and magazines. A book-case, bamboo, with a few ancient novels — mostly Edgar Wallace — detective stories or biographies — a man's taste. No romance — Rick Morrell barred that. A leopard-skin hung over one solitary easy chair. Rick had shot the animal in the mountains. A few Africa native war implements hung on the walls for ornament. A room with a barbaric touch and not a single feminine luxury.

Yet Gay was glad to be here, to be away from that sinister hotel and Mulheim's covetous eyes. When Rick

Morrell brought her here he had shown her into the bedroom that adjoined this living-room; another badly furnished room with a single bed in a mosquito cage, and every evidence that the black servants in his employ neglected their work and got away with it.

Rick Morrell, who had been the most fastidious of men, well turned out and proud of his mother's charming flat, had got to the pitch where he didn't care about anything or anybody in the world. And Gay Burnett knew it, and regretted the fact for his sake.

As soon as they got here his first thought was for a drink. He clapped his hands peremptorily for his 'boy' and ordered a gin-sling.

Gay sat by the open window, leaning back in the chair with closed eyes, trying to forget how badly her head ached after this wretched day, and to keep the tears from her eyes when she visualized the future. Now and then she turned to look at the Englishman who had rescued her from Kurt Mulheim.

How restless he was, a queer, tormented soul, pacing up and down this room. He

had the leonine grace of a jungle animal
. . . up and down . . . up and down. With
pity and bewilderment in her gaze, she
watched. She found herself pitying him.
If only he would stop drinking! He was
splendid to look at still. As he passed
her chair, she looked up and saw the
bronze column of his throat about the
open shirt-collar; the thickness of his
crisp brown hair. There was something
boyish and lovable about Rick's head.
But there were smouldering fires in his
bitter, hazel eyes, with nothing of youth
in them.

"Why don't you sit down?" she asked
him suddenly.

He turned to her. It was on the tip of
his tongue to tell her that he regretted
bringing her to his bungalow; that the
sight of her, sitting there in that chair,
reopened an old wound that had not
healed. For Lydia might have sat by the
window in his home in just such a way,
and he resented the sight of Gay's golden
head and pale, tired young face. Damn
it, she revived old hopes, old ambitions
best left slumbering.

If Lydia had married him . . . she

might have been with him tonight, like
Gay. But their home would have been
fresh and clean and full of flowers, and
her lips would have been his to kiss, her
lovely little body his to hold . . .

Damn women!

Gay, without knowing what passed in
his tormented mind, gave him a faint,
timid smile.

"Would you rather I went to bed?"

He answered:

"I don't care what you do."

His rough voice brought the colour to
her cheeks. He was difficult. She did not
know what to make of him. But she did
know that it was that bottle of gin that
was altering him rapidly from the kind,
chivalrous man who had talked politics
so sanely and brought her here, into
the 'drunken sot' that Mulheim had
labelled him.

"If only I could keep him from the
bottle — interest him," she thought.
She said:

"Tell me about Liberia, Rick."

He went on pacing up and down the
room again, clinging on to his glass. He
avoided looking at her.

"There's nothing to tell . . . except that it's a poisonous place with a poisonous climate . . . enough to rot a man's soul."

"The heat is killing," she said. "I'm very anxious to get back to England."

"England!" he echoed, and lifted his glass and drained it. "Ye gods, I shall never see England's white cliffs again."

"Why not?"

He looked at her sulkily.

"Because I'm chained here to this damned place."

"Is any human being chained?"

"Yes," he said. "I've gone to the dogs, my dear, and I know it, and I can't get back . . . to England . . . I'm the black, black sheep now, damned and all that. Haven't you read your Kipling?"

"You haven't really gone to the dogs," she said patiently.

"I don't know what you call it, then."

"You make yourself out worse than you are . . . "

"Are you making yourself out better than *you* are?" he sneered. "Women have a habit of doing that."

Gay flushed. At any other time if a man had spoken to her so, she would have walked out of the room. But she wanted to stay and talk to Rick. She knew there was goodness and decency in him and that he was trying to check it, to allow the alcohol to rouse the demons in him again. She was curiously interested in him — thrilled and unafraid.

"Do you take it for granted that I am bad?" she asked with a wry little smile.

"All women are . . . "

"That's absurd — just because one woman let you down."

"Lydia was like you."

"But I hope I'm not like Lydia."

"Nobody can tell — those big innocent eyes, that clear baby voice — all very deceptive," he said, and laughed.

"You've lost your real sense of humour," said Gay, and waited for him to blaze at her, but he said nothing, only laughed again. Through his drink-inflamed mind ran the question:

"*Is* she angel or devil . . . isn't she trying to get the better of me . . . for her own ends?"

Footsteps on the wooden verandah outside the bungalow broke the silence

66

of the night. Gay jumped to her feet and her face paled.

"Is that Mulheim . . . ?"

"No, not he," said Rick. "Some fellows I know — traders — come for me."

"Come for you?"

"Oh yes — " He drained his glass again. "The night is young. The saloons are only just waking up in this benighted town. It's the time to go out and get really going."

Gay's heart sank. Surely he wasn't going to go out and drink more. Her heart ached with pity and dismay. He was too fine for this, too nice. If only she could stop him, appeal to him.

Two men — both older than Rick Morrell — tough colonials — strolled into the living room. They had both 'dined well'. They greeted Rick uproariously.

"Here's how, old fellow — coming out? Come on. There's going to be fun in Li Ching's bar tonight, I hear . . . "

"Sorry if we're in the way, pal," said one of them, eyeing Gay with frank curiosity. "Didn't know you had a girl friend with you, Morry."

"I'm just coming, boys," said Rick;

"join you in a moment."

The men looked at Gay again, smiled significantly, and walked out.

Gay faced Rick Morrell, her cheeks flushing and paling, her hands locked nervously together.

"Rick," she said, "you aren't really going, are you?"

"Why shouldn't I?" He finished his drink and straightened his collar and tie. "I always do."

"But it's so late — "

"Rubbish, child. The night's only beginning. Besides, I want to forget that women like you exist."

She flinched, but Gay did not lack courage. She drew closer to the Englishman and lifted a determined young face.

"Don't go — please."

For an instant he stared at her in amazement. She did not lower that proud, fair head. She was thinking:

"I may be able to save him — help him — I want to because he saved me — "

And he was thinking:

"Great God, isn't she like Lydia . . . ?"

Then he burst out laughing, grimly.

"Don't go, eh? Not have my usual

merry round . . . not get carried to bed by Mamba? And why ever not, my dear?"

"Because I ask it," she said, "I want you to stay with me."

Rick Morrell stared and stopped laughing. Then he put a hand to his bloodshot eyes. The drink he had been taking all the evening was distorting his perspective, drowning his best impulses. He saw Gay in an entirely erroneous light. He saw her not as an innocent, decent girl trying to reclaim him . . . but as a wanton, a little adventuress, like Lydia . . . anxious to enslave him with her charms, then throw him over and make him suffer afresh. And he went mad with anger. But mixed with rage was passion. The whole evening, ever since he had brought her here, the beauty, the sweetness of this girl had been creeping into his blood. And he knew that he wanted her, crazily . . . as he had wanted Lydia. But Lydia he had respected because he meant to marry her.

This little actress didn't want him to go down town: she wanted him to stay with her, did she? Very well.

He turned on his heel and went out on the verandah. Gay, her heart beating violently, heard him say:

"Not tonight, boys. I'm staying in . . . "

She was glad about that, but she didn't like the significance of the loud laughter from the others. Then Rick came back. He was smiling, white about the lips, and there was a new, strange, hot look in his handsome eyes.

He came straight up to her, and to her dismay caught her in his arms.

"So you are like all the rest," he said thickly. "It wasn't for safety you came here with me, my little white and gold rose of a girl. It was because you wanted an *English* protector. Well, I'm flattered. And I'm only too willing to protect you. But not from myself."

"No — oh no!" Gay said indignantly. "*No!* You are making a mistake, honestly you are!"

But the last protest was smothered, for Rick laughed again and then bent his head and set his lips to her mouth.

4

GAY struggled against that embrace, that long, deep kiss; struggled until her whole body seemed to ache, to throb with pain. She resented it fiercely, and she was bitterly disappointed in this man. She had believed in the good that lay in his soul; she had trusted him.

She ought to hate him now — despise him for this. *Ought to!* But deep down in her heart she could not. Could not shrink with repulsion from the passion of his arms and lips, as she had done with Kurt Mulheim. Why? She was much too confused, too upset, to analyse her emotions. She was conscious only of a queer shame because something in her thrilled to this man's embrace.

Even while she found him, her blood leaped through her veins. She twined her head to elude his lips. He laughed and kissed her throat. She said through her teeth:

"Brute . . . beast!"

"Isn't it what you've asked for?" he demanded. He was flushing, panting; his arms still held her a helpless captive. "You little golden-haired thing — your lips are honey-sweet — you're slender and supple as a young birch in my arms. I could love you. *Could*. But, my God, I'm not going to! Never again, my dear. Once was enough. I adored every hair of Lydia's lovely head. Then she chucked me. How long do *you* want me for your lover, little Gay? Just for a day, a night — or more?"

He laughed again and buried his lips in the tumbled silk of her hair. The frightened pulse in her throat leaped beneath his kisses.

"Don't!" she said faintly. "Don't . . . *please!*"

"But you asked me to stay — "

"Not for this. You *can't* believe that . . . Rick Morrell," she panted his name, her eyes blazing up at him. "You're mad! You know you are. Mad — or just drunk!"

"No, I'm quite sober. I'm all ready for love, and I haven't loved anybody since

72

Lydia left me. Only this time we start quits. We'll agree to chuck each other when we're tired of it. Yes, *darling?*"

He was threading his fingers through her hair. Her resistance snapped. She ceased to struggle. White as death, she lay motionless against him. But the blueness of her eyes — dark with passionate resentment — still blazed up at him. She had not one clear thought left in her brain. Those caressing fingers were driving her mad, and she wanted to loathe him and could not. He was as tender now as a lover should be; there was witchery in his voice, his touch. It sapped her vitality, even while she sensed the contempt behind it all. She began to realize for the first time what a physical attraction could be like. A thing she had never before experienced.

"Lovely curly hair . . . so like Lydia's. Hers was redder, of course. But her lips were not as sweet and magical as yours. Nor had she that divine hollow in her throat. Let me kiss it again, my sweet . . . so!"

Gay grew calm and very cold. She put both her small hands against his chest and with all her force pushed him away. She stood there, very straight and brave and defiant, before him. She said:

"Rick Morrell, you're crazy and you're drunk, and you're damning your immortal soul. Stop it! *Stop it*, I say! You'd better — if you don't want to die with this sort of thing on your conscience."

Silence a moment. He laughed and brushed a thick lock of brown hair back from his forehead. The sweat ran down his brown cheeks. His eyes were flaming. But the laughter broke queerly, and suddenly he grew serious. It was as though that cool little voice and the sight of that defiant, courageous young figure, tore down the red mists that drink and passion had thrown across his vision. He put a hand to his lips.

"So you don't want me to make love to you, eh?"

"No," she said, and prayed God he would go before she broke down and cried. She felt that she would be lost if she began to weep in front of him.

He drew a hand across his eyes. Then he staggered to the open window.

"Oh, God," he muttered. "What have I

done? I don't know. I think you're right. I'm crazy. The drink has sent me quite mad."

Gay looked in panic at the broad back turned to her. Then she seized her opportunity. She made a bolt for the bedroom door, opened it, stumbled into the room and shut the door behind her. She stood still a moment, and then hid her face in her hands. The tears came now, pouring down her cheeks.

The man in the verandah heard her crying. He was filled with self-loathing and with bitterness.

"I'm not going to believe in her and be duped again. She's a fine little actress — like Lydia. But she was plucky, by God — she was game — and dead right about me," he thought.

He felt that he must get away from this bungalow and the sound of the girl's sobbing. He walked to the shed which served as a garage, wound up his car and drove off furiously into the night.

Lying face downwards on the bed which was his, Gay cried until she was sick and blind.

"How could he — how could he?" she

sobbed again and again.

But through all her humiliation and misery there came, against all effort to choke it, the thrilling memory of those magnetic fingers threading through her tumbled hair and her inexplicable response that had stirred in her blood at the touch of his lips.

She thought feverishly:

"Tomorrow I will go to the Consul and get away. I *must* get away from this terrible place and from him . . . from *myself!*"

It was late when she managed to close her eyes and sleep. And then she did not undress. She lay, fully clothed, on Rick Morrell's bed, and dozed, starting and waking at every sound.

It must have been about three o'clock in the morning that she heard the hum and throb of a car coming at a reckless pace up to the bungalow. She woke up then, with every nerve in her body jumping, and sat on the edge of the bed, listening; her cheeks fiery hot, her heart pounding.

Rick had come home. He would be far from sober; she knew that. Probably he would come in here. She felt suffocated and sick with suspense.

She heard clumsy, staggering footsteps on the steps; stumbling footsteps along the verandah. She waited and listened, a hand to her throat. But the footsteps did not come in her direction. They vanished, and there was peace and silence again.

He had come home, but was not coming in here to terrify her. Relief brought the tears back to Gay's eyes. She lay down with her face buried in the pillow and once more sobbed herself into an uneasy slumber.

When she awoke again the sun was shining, and she found the bungalow deserted. Mamba, the houseboy, who spoke tolerable English, told her that the master had gone out. He usually met the traders on business at this, the coolest hour of the day.

Gay was unutterably thankful. She did not want to face Rick again. She made up her mind to run away before he came back.

5

KURT MULHEIM stood on the verandah of the hotel which had housed the film company until yesterday, and in which he was now the only one left.

Gay had gone. Mulheim realized that with unspeakable rage in his soul. When he had struggled on to his feet after that knock-out blow from the Englishman, Kurt had gone to the bathroom, bathed the blood from his face and put a piece of sticking-plaster on his jaw. He presented an unattractive spectacle with that bruised, swelling jaw and a livid face, but he knew *that* would soon get right again.

It was Gay he worried about. She had gone, and he wanted her. He meant to get her, too, at any cost. In this savage, primitive country, many wild and lawless deeds were done, and Mulheim, all his own unscrupulous and brutal nature roused, intended to get possession of Gay Burnett by foul means if he failed by fair.

"First, I'd like to murder that Englander — Richard Morrell — damn him for his interference," Mulheim reflected. "I'd like to have him locked up in a concentration camp in my country. And Gay, she shall realize that she can't get away from me, now that I have offered her marriage."

It did not take him long to discover that Gay had gone over to the Englishman's bungalow. Yes, Gay was to be found there obviously. Mulheim had made enquiries, and he knew exactly where Rick's home was located. Less than five miles from the bazaar. The burning question was how to get hold of Gay without encountering Morrell again. Mulheim's jaw ached and smarted, and he was not willing to risk another blow from that powerful fist.

What the devil could he do?

While he stood there, staring angrily into the hot, starry night, a woman came out of the hotel and stood an instant on the verandah, looking at him discreetly. Mulheim immediately turned his attention to her. He did

not remember having seen her before.
He was at once struck by her strange
resemblance to Gay Burnett. She was
a little older, of course, and had harder
features, a more sensual mouth, and her
hair was a flaming red. She had the
same fair skin and wide blue eyes and
fragile, appealing air that had attracted
Kurt to Gay. This girl looked chic, even
theatrical, in appearance. She wore a silk
shirt, white breeches, and riding-boots,
and carried a crop in her hand.

She continued to eye him covertly,
then took a cigarette from a case. The
German seized his chance and leaped to
her side with a match. And even while
he lit the cigarette and she murmured her
thanks, he jumped to wild conclusions
about her. She must be Lydia Brett.
The woman who had jilted Rick Morrell.
Everybody out here knew Morrell's story.

"Pardon me," said Mulheim in his
heavy guttural voice, "but are you not
— Miss Brett?"

She smiled and raised delicate brows.

"I *was*. How did you know? I'm Mrs.
Milcroft now."

"Ah, yes!"

"You've heard of me?"

"Who hasn't?"

The German knew how to pay compliments. A few moments later he and the girl were sitting side by side, drinking, smoking, and they soon knew quite a lot about each other.

Mulheim heard that Lydia was now a widow. Old Roger Milcroft had died some months ago, and left her most of his fortune. She was free and rich, and she had come to Liberia. Why? Oh, she wanted to see an old friend . . . just one friend in particular. And then, of course, it leaked out. Lydia Milcroft had traveled thousands of miles from New York to this outlandish spot, because she wanted to see Rick Morrell. She had regretted losing him, She wanted to renew their old affair. And she had heard from their acquaintances in London that he was out here drinking himself into the grave. For love of her. So flattering!

Mulheim gleaned all the information he required about the beautiful little Lydia. Enough to convince him that she was a pagan, heartless young woman whose beauty masked a scheming and mercenary spirit. He was not a young idiot to be duped by her. He saw that now she had the money, she wanted the old lover back. She put it so sweetly. She must save him from drink, and make him happy again, poor sweet, she said.

But Lydia Milcroft never really wanted to make anybody but herself happy. It was just that her former passion for handsome Rick Morrell was in her blood. She *wanted* him. That was all. Could Mr. Mulheim tell her anything about Rick?

Mulheim told her quite a lot — much that was not strictly true. He enlarged on the story of last night. He accused Morrell of 'taking his woman'.

"You see," he finished with a gesture of his hand that held his famous meerschaum pipe, "Gay Burnett really belongs to me. She came out with my company on the understanding that she would become my wife eventually."

Lydia's brilliant eyes — so much harder and colder than the warm, soft eyes of Gay — narrowed in the darkness and she smiled to herself. She fancied that she knew this man Mulheim. He was of a political value — a Nazi agent. But of no consequence to her. And it was, of course, not at all true that Gay belonged to him. She was aware of that. But it suited Lydia's purpose to believe every word Mulheim had to say.

"It's too bad," she murmured. "The girl must be a little brute to run away from you like that — when you've been so kind to her. I'm sure if Rick knew her true character he would not want her in his bungalow."

"No, of course not," agreed Mulheim. "You see what has happened? She has told Mr. Morrell tales — erroneous ones, of course — about me, and he considered it his duty to offer Gay his protection."

"Misplaced chivalry," murmured Lydia, and smiled again, wickedly, secretly, as she noted the purple bruise and the plaster on Mulheim's heavy jowl. She could guess that it was Rick who was responsible for the German's injuries.

"It appears to me," added Mulheim, "that Mr. Morrell will be most glad to see you again — to get you back, if I might put it that way — " He bowed with exaggerated courtesy. "We have all heard the story. And the little Gay will be — what shall we call it? — the third who never makes good company."

Lydia was not smiling now. Her red lips were a thin line, and Mulheim knew that not a word from this woman could be called strictly true. But he saw in Lydia a very important ally. A woman who wanted the Englishman, Morrell, and would, therefore, be anxious to get Gay Burnett away from him.

Lydia, in her turn, listened to the guttural voice of the German and heard what he had to tell her about Gay. She was none too pleased to discover that there was a pretty English girl out here ready to console Rick. No! That did not suit Lydia's book at all. The wealthy, spoiled widow of the late Roger Milcroft wanted her old lover back again.

"That girl mustn't stay with Rick," she said to Mulheim. "It won't suit either of our ends — will it?"

"Quite so. Supposing we have another drink," he said, his eyes beaming through the thick lenses, "and think out a little plan for getting Miss Burnett away from your — er — friend, Mr. Morrell."

Lydia was ready and willing to have the drink and make the 'little plan'. She knew Ricks' nature. She was going to have a difficult task to regain his lost faith in her. And she did not want a girl younger and prettier than herself in the way. Oh no — that wouldn't suit her at all. She raised her glass and said carelessly:

"*Heil Hitler!*"

The German glowed and returned the toast fervently.

She sat talking to him until the early hours of the morning. Just after sunrise the next day, before the hot sun had time to torture the baked earth and the gasping citizens of the West African town, Lydia Milcroft drove in a handsome Buick car to Rick Morrell's bungalow.

She had made enquires and discovered that it was the habit of her former lover to go out at this comparatively cool hour and meet some of the coastal travellers and the natives with whom he traded ivories.

Lydia banked on Rick being out when she arrived at the bungalow, and fortune favoured her. She found the place deserted except for the black 'boys' and a young fair-haired girl with a tired, unhappy face. She wore a blue linen suit, carried a bag and hat in her hand, and looked as though she were about to make a journey. With the utmost curiosity Lydia studied this girl who was said to resemble herself.

Gay had made up her mind to run away from Rick just as she had run from Mulheim, to reach the British Consulate and arrange for her passage to a more civilized part of Africa if not to England, and be out of both men's clutches. She had not seen Rick since last night. Now, while he was out on business, she could get away. But how, she did not know. She was staring at the desolate country around Rick's bungalow in despair, wondering how to find a car, when Lydia's magnificent tourer rolled up to the house. Her heart leaped with joy at the sight of an Englishwoman in that car beside the native driver.

Lydia stepped down from the car and advanced to the verandah. She gave Gay her most charming smile.

"Is Mr. Morrell at home?" she asked sweetly.

"No," said Gay. "I — my name's Gay Burnett. Who are you?"

"Mrs. Milcroft is my name. So *very* sorry Rick's out . . . he's a very old friend of mine . . . "

"Oh yes," said Gay. She neither knew nor cared who or what Lydia was. She did not even pause to wonder whether this fair-haired, blue-eyed woman was Rick's former fiancée and the one responsible for his moral downfall. She only knew that Lydia was an Englishwoman and had a car.

"Mrs. Milcroft," said Gay breathlessly, "I hope you don't mind my asking, but could you *possibly* give me a lift into town — to the British Consulate?"

Lydia smiled. This was easier than she or Kurt Mulheim had anticipated, and just what they had both hoped for. No need to lie, to persuade the girl into going with her. She seemed only too frantically anxious to get away from Rick's bungalow — little idiot.

"Of course I'll give you a lift," she said.

"Come right along. I'll take you now if you're ready."

"It's awfully good of you," said Gay, and gave a great sigh of relief as she joined Lydia in the car.

Once she was driving away from the bungalow she gave it a quick, backward look. Her heart jumped queerly as she thought of Rick's fierce kisses. She thought:

"He could have been . . . *wonderful*. I shall never be able to forget . . . it's all such a tragedy . . . but I'm glad to get away . . ."

Yet, was she as glad as all that? Or was there a faint twinge of regret in her heart because she would never see Rick Morrell again? Gay refused to analyse her feelings too deeply. She turned her attention to her new 'friend'. Lydia was putting one or two leading questions.

"How is Rick these days?"

"Oh — I — I would really rather not discuss him," said Gay in an embarrassed way.

"Don't you like him?"

"I really don't know him at all well," blurted out Gay.

Lydia gave her a swift, sidelong look, saw the girl's cheeks were crimson and thought she understood. But she was not jealous. She thought that she had no need to be. She continued to talk smoothly and kindly to Gay.

"You poor dear — I'm afraid you haven't had a very good time lately. Men are such brutes . . . I know old Rick was always fond of women. I daresay he rather scared you last night — didn't he? I know him so well!" She laughed significantly.

Gay fell into the trap.

"He did scare me a little," she said. "And I agree with you. I think men are *beasts!*"

Then Lydia knew what she wanted to know. Rick had made love to this girl. That was enough for Lydia. Gay Burnett was much too pretty and appealing, and Gay must be got out of Rick's way. Lydia told the chauffeur to step hard on the accelerator of the car.

It appeared to Gay that they were travelling a long distance down the white dusty road and through wild country fringed by native plantations. It was quite a different route from the one she had taken with Rick last night. But she did not know the country and did not begin to suspect that anything was wrong for a considerable time. Mrs. Milcroft was English and had promised to take her to the Consulate, and why should she doubt her?

She had not the least idea where the Consulate was. Lydia Milcroft assured her that she knew this coastal town well, knew all Liberia, in fact, and would take Gay by the shortest possible route.

But Lydia did nothing of the sort. She drove the girl whom Kurt Mulheim wanted twenty-five miles away from the town to a rest-house which was situated on the palm-fringed border of the Congo plains. A place owned by a friend of Mulheim's. A German with black blood in him. He was known as Manuel. Manuel ran this apology of an hotel for traders from all parts of the coast and made some of his money selling raw Cape spirit which was smuggled to him, but most of it by selling slaves in the secret slave market in the desert whence native boys and girls were shipped to all part of Africa. A primitive concern out of reach and out of sight of the civilized dwellers on the Gold Coast.

Manuel was of darkish skin, but he might have been a Spaniard or Italian. Even his eyes were blue. Only his thick lips and finger-nails gave away his half-caste blood. He could be very pleasant when he chose. He was popular with everybody, but under the mask he was one of the most cunning criminals in Africa, and in the pay of Germany.

It was to this astonishing place that Mulheim had told Lydia to bring Gay. Both women stared in some astonishment at the long, low white building which stood raised a little off the ground with a long step running round it, on the very edge of the naked desert. Behind lay the dense, sinister growth of jungle.

Gay turned to her new-found woman friend.

"Is *this* the Consulate?" she asked.

Lydia made no reply. Now that she had brought Gay Burnett here, she was a little scared of her own action. The chauffeur had pulled the Buick up before the rest-house and was blowing the horn.

She hoped Mulheim would come quickly and take charge of the girl. There was something so fresh and sweet about Gay that made even Lydia, adventuress though she was, feel a trifle ashamed of the dirty trick she had played on her.

Gay, however, remained entirely unsuspicious until Manuel, the German proprietor, emerged from the hotel and greeted the two women. He wore spotless white ducks and a topee. He bade Lydia and Gay welcome, but regretted, he said, that Mr. Mulheim had sent a native with a message that he was delayed on important business and could not reach the rest-house until noon.

"Damn!" said Lydia under her breath. "What are we going to do with this girl?"

Manuel smoothed his upper lip and glanced at Gay. She was sitting in the car like one paralysed. She had heard what Manuel had said and her face was white as a sheet. Her heart had given a sick jerk, and begun to beat violently as she realized that this was *not* the British Consulate, and that it was into the hands of the German that she had fallen.

Manuel came slowly towards her, smiling. She thought she had never seen a more sinister smile or a more sinister figure than the negroid-German made in his immaculate European clothes. She jumped out of the car and ran forward with a cry.

"Mrs. Milcroft — you — *surely* . . . "

The words died in her throat. For Lydia had climbed into the Buick and was letting in the clutch.

"Sorry!" she said. "So long! Keep her, Manuel. It'll be more than your life's worth to let her go till Mulheim comes."

Gay stared at her like one transfixed with fear. The chauffeur had flung her suitcases out on to the ground. The car was moving away. Then Gay screamed at Lydia.

"Mrs. Milcroft — for God's sake — Mrs. Milcroft — don't leave me — !"

But Lydia was anxious to be out of it. She did not like it, nor her part in this dastardly deed. The Buick was spinning down the dusty road and vanished from sight, leaving a cloud of white dust.

Gay gave an anguished cry and would

have run after the car, but Manuel's hand held her arm gently but firmly, and pulled her up the step into the rest-house out of the blazing sunshine.

"No use," he said in good English. "The lady has gone. You must stay with me, Fräulein. And you must not get sun-stroke. Mr. Mulheim would not like that, *hein?*"

Gay wrenched her arm from his fingers.

"You're a friend of Mr. Mulheim's," she said hysterically. "You're all in league with him to get me here. But it's illegal. The British police will search for me — find me. You can't do things like this — "

She stopped, a sob in her throat, and looked wildly round her. But she saw only the black, grinning face of negro servants. Not another white face.

The eyes of Manuel followed her appraisingly. His cunning brain seethed with thoughts. He did not know much about this English girl. He was in the pay of the German. Mulheim's orders were law. He would keep her here if Mulheim paid. But the pay was never much, and Manuel knew where he would get five or even six times that price. *By putting the fair girl up for sale* in the great secret market in the desert.

Gay looked at him wildly.

"Whoever you are, help me get to the British Consul," she said, "and I'll see that you get a handsome reward."

Manuel looked furtively round him, smiled and nodded.

"I would not dream of detaining you, Fräulein," he said softly. "If you will come with me in my car, I will drive you at once back to town. I had no idea that you were brought here by force. I am a friend of the Consul's. You can count on me. Come along."

Gay, with the merest shred of faith left in mankind, followed the half-caste, knowing that she had no choice but to trust him, wondering in horror if she would ever awaken from the nightmare which had pursued her since Iris Power left her alone in the hotel.

6

IT took Gay exactly an hour to realize that once again she had been tricked. And this time, condemned to a fate worse than any she had imagined in her most terrible dreams. No nightmare could have been more sinister, more dreadful. No book that she had read, nor film that she had seen, could have equalled *this*.

The man Manuel drove her in a closed car — at breakneck speed — not to the Consulate, but many long miles in the opposite direction, far into the desert — those burning plains of Liberia where few white men are seen.

Gay, sitting at Manuel's side, stared at the scenery which grew every mile more desolate and more barbaric, and very soon had a shrewd idea at the back of her head that this man was doing to her what Lydia had done.

"This is not the way back to town," she said several times. "It *can't* be."

Each time, Manuel smiled and answered:

"Oh, but it is — I assure you. Have no fear, Fräulein."

When they had covered twenty miles, Gay became certain that Manuel was tricking her. Cold and shaking, she pulled at his arm so violently that the car swerved in its course.

"Stop, stop at once!" she said. "I don't want to go on!"

Then the man showed his true colours. He pulled up the car and turned to her with an ugly look on his face.

"Oh — so you don't want to go on — and why?"

Her heart seemed to stop beating.

"Because I feel certain this isn't the way to the town," she said, and looking round her dizzily. Where had she come? Nothing in sight but burning, sandy plain, a few clumps of palm trees, cactus, flowering in wild splendour, and in the distance the dark frowning shadow of some sinister jungle.

She heard a low laugh and then her wrists were caught and chained before she could move. Half-dead with fright,

Gay Burnett stared at the chains . . . like small, silver bracelets . . . *handcuffs*.

"What are you doing? What is it you mean to do?"

He laughed again, stooped, and with an incredibly quick movement seized both her ankles and snapped something about them. Gay realized, then, that her feet as well as her hands were chained together.

Manuel — shaking with laughter — drove on. Gay screamed at him — hysterical with fright — nerves and courage failing her.

"What are you doing? Why have you put these things on me? In heaven's name, where are you taking me?"

His answer reached her, brutal and without attempt at courting friendliness this time.

"Not to the Consulate, little English lady. But to Ligati."

This name conveyed nothing to her.

"Where is Ligati? What is it?" she gasped.

"It is the one and only slave market left in this part of the world," he replied, and laughed again.

Gay — half fainting — sat back in her seat and stared blindly at the man. Drops of moisture rolled down her cheeks. She could not yet quite grasp the terrible significance of what Manuel said.

"A slave market?" she whispered stupidly, and then added. "Don't be ridiculous. Such things don't exist any longer."

"Yes," he said, "here they do. I was paid by Herr Mulheim to keep you in my hotel for marriage with him, but I shall be paid a good deal more by one of the dealers in the Ligati market when you are put up for auction. You are so pretty, English girl, with your golden hair and milk-white skin."

A mist came across Gay's eyes, a frightful sensation of horror seized her.

Put up for auction . . . in a slave market . . . Oh, God, what was the evil creature saying? It couldn't be true.

Then she saw that they were reaching some kind of village, a native settlement, brown huts under the shade of tall palms and feathery date trees. An African village in the desert waste.

This was Ligati . . . A village, had

Gay known it, peopled by a fierce tribe of pure-blooded Negroes, and visited by men from all over the Far East. Japs, Mongolians, Chinese. Never white men. If a white man came, he was allowed to go his way unmolested, but never to see the auction sales of men and women in the market square. A great square in a clearing, in which stood a platform covered with a gay, striped scarlet awning. On that platform, every week, a few hundred slaves were put up to auction — bought and sold.

Merchants and traders of savage tribes swarmed here to purchase men for servants, and women for wives.

It seemed incredible to Gay as she began to realize the facts that here, within fifty miles of a civilized town, there was a slave market such as had existed thousands of years ago. Gold passed from hands to hands — miserable young children were torn from their parents — girls from their sweethearts — husbands from their wives.

And into this seething, palpitating cauldron of enslaved humanity came Gay Burnett, half-mad with terror, yet able to see and think and understand exactly the ghastly thing that was happening to her.

Better, far, if she had stayed with Mulheim, she thought. And far better had she never left Rick Morrell's bungalow. What would Rick have thought of *this*, she wondered hysterically.

She was dragged from the car by a giant Negro on to the platform. There she was pushed into a heap of women; chained together, awaiting auction. She thought she would die of shame, of terror. Yet she lived and suffered all the agonies of suspense, of not knowing what her fate would be.

She asked herself again and again in that dark hour, what Rick would have said. Of course, he would have saved her. And she found herself with pale, dry lips, murmuring his name.

"Rick . . . Rick Morrell . . . Rick Morrell, come and save me!"

Manuel stood in a crowd of traders, smoking, watching, chatting with a mixture of nationalities. Wealthy Chinamen and Japs, Negro kings with most of the gold of their country at their disposal, fierce Slavs, and traders from Malaya and

101

India. They chattered and laughed and preened their heads to see what women were for sale today.

On the platform, exhausted, stricken with fear, Gay Burnett huddled with the other girls. They took no notice of her. They were concerned with their own personal misery. Fair Circassians; olive-skinned Mexicans; chocolate and bronze-limbed natives. But Gay was the only woman there of pure white blood. And Manuel had guessed that her golden hair, blue eyes and her education would fetch an enormous price.

A great gong reverberated through the market-place and silence fell upon the crowd. The traders pressed forward. A very old skinny native woman pulled Gay forward, separating her from the rest. Shuddering in every limb, she realized that she was to be sold first.

Her hat was taken from her and the gold silk of her hair revealed. Her arms were stretched out to show the ivory whiteness of her skin. Traders pressed forward and touched her dainty feet and silk-shod ankles curiously. A European was not to be bought every day.

The auction began. Gay understood nothing, only guessed that large prices were being offered for her. To her intense horror, she also realized that a tall Chinaman with a silk umbrella over him was one of the highest bidders.

She gave a little moan of despair. She began to wonder how she could kill herself before she was given into the yellow hands of that Oriental. Then suddenly the blood rushed to her livid face and hope returned to her heart. For she heard a voice bidding side by side with the Chinaman's . . . a deep, familiar, drawling voice . . . *an English voice.* But the man who spoke knew native dialect and used it. Her swimming eyes searched his face and recognized Rick Morrell. He looked up at her, growing horror in his eyes. She sobbed aloud:

"Rick, Rick!" and could only thank God that he was here and hope now for her release from this nightmare.

"Ssh . . . nobody knows I'm English," he said. "But I'll buy you — if I can!" he whispered to her. "But the bidding is high, and God knows what'll happen if I can't go on . . . and if I don't get away from here in time to get help for you."

She kept her gaze riveted on him. The sweat poured down her face. She stood like a statue of despair . . . listening to the shouts and cries of the market . . . heard first the Chinaman's metallic voice, then Rick's deep one, then the auctioneer, spurring them on in a language which she could not understand.

"Oh, God, Rick — save me!" she moaned.

He looked up at her.

"The Chink's determined to have you," he said hoarsely. "Gay, it's no use. I've no more money. *I can't go on!*"

7

SHE gave a long cry of despair.
"You must go on — Rick — you
must!"
The old native woman was half
supporting her now. Her limbs shook
so that she could scarcely stand. She
only half-saw the sea of dark, eager
faces staring up at her, the swarm
of traders — black, yellow, half-caste
— surging round the platform. For
Gay there were only two figures on
which she focused clearly. First and
foremost, the tall, gracefully built one
of Rick in his disguise. Nobody would
have taken him for a European. He had
blackened his already brown face to an
ebony black, and a turban was wound
around his head. She could see that he
was sober enough now, in all conscience.
Fully alive to the frightfulness of the
transaction taking place on that platform.
The other figure, the Chinaman, a man
almost as tall as Rick, had a face that

might have been carved of old ivory. Inscrutable, almond-shaped, opaque eyes; long, terrible hands with gold-encased nails showing that he was of high degree. He was a brilliant figure amongst the white-clad natives. He wore a long loose robe of gold-embroidered, jade-green silk and was hatless. But the silk umbrella — a queer symbol of Westernism — protected the oil black head, with its long pig-tail, from the sun.

Those two men alone, amongst all the traders, had been bidding for Gay Burnett for the last ten minutes. The rest had dropped out. And now the bidding had stopped altogether. The auctioneer was speaking to Rick. He was answering hotly, furiously, his face livid. Had Gay been able to understand she would have heard him say:

"I warn you, you miserable scoundrel — if you let this English girl be sold into the hands of that yellow bastard, the whole British Government will come down and wipe you out of existence. I am English. English — do you hear?"

The Chinaman — hearing and understanding the none too polite name which he had been called, narrowed his eyes to slits. But he laughed softly and fanned himself with a tiny lace fan.

"Tee! . . . hee! . . . hee!"

The auctioneer — a great mulatto — a little scared by this revelation of the unknown's nationality — looked at Manuel. Manuel, knowing that he was about to get a big price for Gay — a far bigger one than he had hoped for — waved him to go on.

"Let this so-called Englishman stew in his own juice. His Government cannot harm us — they have no authority in Ligati. Let the girl be sold."

"Rick — Rick!" Gay's anguished voice echoed through the market-place. For the tall Chinaman was advancing towards the dias and she knew what was happening now. The auctioneer struck a gong. It reverberated through the hot and quivering air. The white girl had been sold. She was moved to one side. A young, slim quadroon, whose liquid black eyes rolled with terror — was pushed forward. Another sale began.

Gay struggled madly in the arms of the old native duenna who was dragging her by her small, chained hands towards the Chinaman.

"No — no — no!"

Rick Morrell stood like one rooted to the spot. He was aghast. Gay Burnett was the property of that yellow chink — a *chink* — whether he was a Mandarin of high degree or not. It was unthinkable. Rick felt he would go mad. But he kept his head — kept it sufficiently to control the violent longing to push through the crowd and get to Gay's side. He knew that would be fatal. Any attempt at a rescue, single-handed, would be madness. He would have no chance in this crowd of savages and ruffians. In Ligati he would just be knifed and finished off and his body thrown to the vultures if he interfered with the sale of a slave.

But that Gay Burnett should be a slave . . . what an iniquitous, incredible thought! He must save her, of course. He would, too. But not by rushing like a bull into a china-shop now. He would go warily, keep quiet, get hold of a fresh disguise and follow Gay wherever her 'owner' took her.

He thanked God that he was here and that he had found out what had happened. When he had returned to his bungalow from his meeting with the ivory traders, this morning, he had been astonished and annoyed to find her gone. The effects of the drinking debauch of the previous night having worn off, Rick felt ashamed of himself. Gay was not as bad as he imagined, and in any case he had no right to insult her so unpardonably. He could not forget the sweetness of her lips and the softness of that timid, shrinking young figure in his arms. He wanted to ask her to forgive him.

A few questions put to his boy had thrown him into a state of perplexity. A white lady had come in a Buick car and driven Gay away? But who was the lady? Then the boy told him. It was a lady, very beautiful, with red hair. Name, Mrs. Milcroft, she had said. That had flung Rick into a state of utter perplexity. *Lydia!* But, good God, why had Lydia come to Africa, *and why had she taken Gay away?*

Perplexed and worried, Rick had driven

into the town. He was determined to see Mulheim and make sure that the German had nothing to do with this particular business. He found Mulheim gone. But a few liberal tips and the native porter at the hotel gave him information. Mr. Mulheim had sent a boy across country with a communication for Manuel. Rick knew Manuel and his ill-famed rest-house. Everybody on the Gold Coast knew about it, though few dared venture there alone. The porter had heard a conversation on the telephone. Mr. Mulheim was meeting two white ladies at Manuel's hotel.

Rick drew his own conclusions from that. The two white ladies must undoubtedly be Gay and Lydia.

Determined to unravel what seemed a complete mystery, Rick drove like one possessed into the wilderness to the borders of the desert where Manuel's rest-house was located.

A few more enquires . . . a little more judicious 'palm oil' enlightened Rick on a few more points. Half-castes are rarely capable of loyalty, and always open to bribery. A servant in the place told the

Englishman that Manuel and a fair-haired English lady had left an hour ago for Ligati.

Not knowing whether he followed Lydia or Gay, but horrified at the idea of either of them travelling with the notorious Manuel to such a spot as Ligati . . . a place which was known as the 'plague-spot' of West Africa . . . Rick followed.

And that was how he found his way here and came to join in the fantastic bidding in the slave market for Gay. The girl who had been brought here was not Lydia, but Gay, who had undoubtedly been the dupe of both Mulheim and Manuel. Just what part Lydia had played in this drama Rick could not begin to fathom.

If only he had known, he told himself again and again, he could have brought more money — all the gold he had in the world — all his ivories — willingly he would have sacrificed his last halfpenny to save that poor little girl from such a fate. But, of course, he would save her, even now.

He looked with bloodshot eyes at the

sight of Gay, struggling for freedom. He saw the Chinaman reach out a hand and take her by the arm . . . then could bear no more. His blood was boiling. He drifted out of sight, away from the seething crowd in the market-place. He knew Manuel's baleful eye was upon him. If Manuel once realized that Rick was a danger he might try and get him quickly and effectively out of the way for good and all.

If he wanted to save Gay, then he must find a way and find it quickly.

He walked through the bazaar of Ligati, a primitive, dirty, noisy thoroughfare. Gold or ivory will buy anything in West Africa. Rick had both in his pockets. He very soon bargained with a toothless old Negro from some second-hand native garments. They were blue cotton, faded and smelly, but they served Rick's purpose. He stripped himself of his clothes, put on the blue cotton shirt and wrapped a long roll of the same material, nativewise, about his loins. A battered straw hat and some sandals made of plaited rush completed the outfit. Rick was darkly brown from the sun, and where the sun had not caught him he stained the fair skin with betel-nut juice. The result was a tall finely-built native, and when he returned to the market-place and joined in the crowd, not a soul would have recognized Rick as the Englishman who had been bidding for the English girl.

Gay thought Rick had deserted her. Her courage, her hope, her last shred of faith in Rick as a friend, deserted her too. She was only half-conscious when the native duenna handed her over to the Chinaman, who, in his turn, gave the man Manuel a leather purse of gold pieces. Gay had fetched a big price in a place where women were often sold for a few shillings.

Li Matin, the Chinaman who now considered himself the legal owner of Gay, was a wealthy Oriental with interests in this country as well as his own. Not many miles from Ligati, there was a settlement, practically composed of Chinese, and known as Quoon. Li Matin had built himself a dwelling-place on Western lines in Quoon, and he was governor of it and of all the people.

He had many females slaves of various nationalities, but no wife. He was a man of some intelligence and learning, and, like many high-caste Chinese, spoke English. He admired the white race, and he had made up his mind to marry a white woman. When, therefore, he had known there was an opportunity to buy, he had come eagerly to Ligati prepared to go to all limits. His one possible rival had dropped out, and Li Matin had won.

He did not, however, intend to treat Gay badly. Indeed, if she was to be his wife, he would treat her with honour, and he told her so. Gay found herself being carried with him in a covered litter, away from the terrible slave market, the memory of which would be a horror to her all her life, and lifted finally on to a white elephant. Li Matin's long arms held her, and she did not struggle. She was past it. She lay weak, exhausted with the heat and terror, listening to what the Chinaman had to say.

"You see, I speak velly good English," he boasted proudly. "I can make you velly good husband."

Husband . . . this man with his yellow

face and slanting eyes . . . Gay shuddered in every limb. Her wild and hopeless eyes stared around her. The white elephant was a big beast, and it seemed to Gay that she saw the country from a great height . . . moving slowly, majestically away from Ligati, across the plains, followed by a score or more of Chinese coolies — some of Li Matin's servants. She felt that she was dead . . . that this was her funeral procession. No — worse than dead . . . Death would have been kinder. If only she *could* die! . . . And Rick had deserted her, or, indeed, been taken prisoner himself.

From her place in the palanquin with Li Matin she could not see a tall figure in blue cotton garments, following in the cloud of dust at the rear of the procession, or she might have known that Rick Morrell, the ivory trader, was close at hand, and that all hope was not yet dead.

"You shall have the robes and jewels of an empress who reigned in Pekin ten thousand years ago," Li Matin murmured in Gay's ear. "You shall have many slaves, and every luxury in my house in Quoon.

Will you then be kind to me, English flower?"

She drew as far from him as she could, moaning:

"No, no! — please take me back to my own people. Let me go back . . . "

Li Matin smiled. He put out a hand as though to touch the tempting yellow silk of her hair. But he resisted temptation. He would not force her. He preferred that his wife come to him willingly. She was frightened . . . all this was strange to her. He would give her time.

"I cannot take you back," he said. "I have brought you and you are mine. You shall have one week, English rose, to grow accustomed to the ways of Quoon, and then you shall marry me according to my rites."

Gay laughed hysterically, went on laughing until the sunlit world revolved about her, and she toppled across the Mandarin in a dead faint.

8

EVENING came. Darkness and quiet after the longest hottest and most terrible day that Gay had ever known.

When the stars — those great, glittering African stars — illuminated the vast sky, Gay found herself alone in Li Matin's guest-room, which had been especially prepared for her. She had been forced to sit with him while he ate his meals, to talk to him and tell him about England. He was insatiable for news. He knew a great deal about modern politics. He wished her to discuss with him the possibilities of a European war. For in one way the man was educated and civilized, and yet in another so hopelessly primitive in her eyes. But now he had left her in peace and told her that she need not fear. She would be unmolested. But her solitary state would last only one week, during which time she must prepare herself for marriage with him.

117

With that knowledge to depress her, Gay was scarcely likely to enjoy her solitude, although she was glad to be alone at last. This was a wonderful room full of exotic treasures. Exquisite lacquer furniture, brought from China, hand-painted screens, silken draperies, a low divan covered with great satin cushions, electrically worked fans revolving above her head ceaselessly, to keep the atmosphere cool.

There were wide open windows leading on to the verandah. But not hope of escape, for the white palace built in the centre of Quoon by Li Matin was surrounded by guards. He had told Gay that it would be futile for her to try to get away. And even if she escaped from the palace, beyond was only a desert in which she would die of heat and thirst. Up and down the verandah walked a sinister figure in uniform. He carried a rifle. He was Gay's own particular guard.

She sat on the divan in that luxurious, gilded prison, stupefied with misery. Li Matin had given her into the hands of two Chinese women she had forced her to bathe in water perfumed and cool, and change her English clothes for a Chinese girl's costume. White satin embroidered trousers and tunic. Lovely costly things. Gay looked fragile and lovely in them, but her great eyes were haunted and sunken in her small face. She wondered what she would do when this week ended and she was forced into marriage with Li Matin, or if she could find some means to kill herself before such a thing could occur. Sometimes she wondered if she had ever lived in peace in her grandfather's gaunt house in the Cotswolds. Dear God, if she could only find herself back there, despite all its discomforts, its loneliness. Why should this fantastic fate have overtaken her?

Li Matin was in his rest-room dreaming over an opium pipe. The village of Quoon lay quiet under the stars. No sound save the occasional wail of a Chinese lute, or the distant throbbing of African drums.

Suddenly Gay fancied she heard the sound of a scuffle, or was it a muffled groan outside her room? She stood up, wide-eyed, apprehensive. Every sound scared her now. Then there was silence again. She tip-toed to the long open window and peered out. She saw only the dripping moonlight through the palm trees, and the tall figure of the guard coming down the verandah towards her. She drew back, shivering.

The guard paused before her. Gay turned to step back into her room. But swiftly he shot out a hand and seized her wrist.

"Ssh! Gay — wait!"

She stood paralysed with astonishment, her heart almost stopping. A perfectly good English voice, and he had said, *"Gay — wait!"*

Then, staring up at the dark face under the brim of the straw hat, she saw, not the usual guard, but Rick Morrell. Rick himself, with a rifle, in the disguise of a poor coolie. She was too astounded to speak for a moment. But she thought she would die of joy and relief. Rick glanced furtively from one side to another.

"Let me into your room. Is it safe?"

"Yes," she said, shivering with wild excitement. "Quickly . . . "

Then he was in her room and she drew silken curtains, shutting out the verandah. She caught his outstretched hands.

"Oh, Rick — Rick — how did you manage it?"

He told her how he had followed the trail of the white elephant from Ligati to Quoon.

"I dared not try and rescue you in Ligati, with that devil Manuel's eye on me," he said, "but I was determined to save you somehow or other. Oh — you poor little thing — what a hellish thing to have happened!"

Quite naturally his arms went round her. She clung to him, tears streaming down her face.

"Rick — it was wonderful of you to come. How did you manage — this?"

"Waited till I saw a chance, then stole into this garden and strangled your guard," he said. "I had to do it. It was the only way."

"So that was what I heard," she whispered.

"Yes. But it isn't safe for me to stay. The thing is — how are we going to get away? I speak a kind of native dialect which they all understand — and my disguise is good — I've got lodging in a Chinese rest-house close by the bazaar. If only I could get you out — "

"You must," said Gay wildly. "You can't let me stay here. Li Matin's only given me a week and then he means to make me marry him, according to his own laws. He is not unkind. He is polite and gentle. But he terrifies me."

Rick looked down at her. He saw not the scheming young woman as he had seen her of his former imagination, but a decent and defenceless English girl in the hands of barbarians. And suddenly he held her close and put his lips against her hair.

"You poor sweet. I must have been mad with drink to do what I did that night," he muttered. "Forgive me . . . "

The closeness of his embrace was suddenly rapture to her. She caught one of his hands and held it fast.

"Don't talk of it now . . . forget it. But let us think of some way of getting out of this terrible place . . . "

"There is no way out . . . save death," said a soft cruel voice with a foreign inflection. "Your pardon, my fiends, if

I put an end to this meeting . . . "

Gay and Rick drew apart. Startled, trembling from head to foot, Gay saw that the curtains had parted and the tall silken-robed figure of Li Martin was framed in the doorway leading on to the verandah. There was a cold, wicked light in his slanting eyes. Gay gave a despairing cry.

"Rick — we're lost — !"

The man's heart sank. Here was a catastrophe indeed. He might have known there was little or no chance of saving Gay. And now he himself was in need of saving, he thought ironically. But what did he matter? It was Gay, the girl, the defenceless woman, who counted.

Li Matin clapped his hands.

Four Chinese boys in uniform and with rifles came with mysterious speed into Gay's room. Li Matin spoke to them. Instantly they seized Rick. He set his teeth and swore, but he knew that it was futile and senseless to resist these men, who were perfect exponents of the art of ju-jutsu — every one of them.

Gay — wild-eyed, panic-stricken — afraid for Rick now, as well as for herself, rushed to Li Matin's side.

"Don't blame him — for heaven's sake don't punish him. He was only trying to save me."

The cold, opaque eyes became slits. Li Matin smiled. He folded his hands in his wide sleeves and bowed.

"Your wishes shall be obeyed. I shall not punish the English dog for the murder of one of my guards, nor for his attempted rescue of his countrywoman. It was natural. But as he is *your lover*, you submit to his kiss . . . " Li Matin snarled the last word. "He is too dangerous a rival to me to be set free. Therefore he shall work in Quoon and cultivate my rice-fields, until he dies a *natural* death."

Gay put a hand to her mouth. Her stricken gaze returned to Rick. He was ghastly pale under the bronze, but he smiled at her.

"That sounds delightful — twenty-four hours' labour out of twenty-four in the sunshine. It will sooner cause a *natural* death . . . Well, the sooner the better. It's you I worry about."

"Oh, my God!" said Gay, and fell on

her knees and covered her face with her hands.

When she looked up, Rick had been taken away. Li Matin, too, had gone. She was alone again. Alone and much more frightened than she had been before. Afraid for *him*. For Rick, who had so gallantly followed and tried to help her and was now going to suffer for his chivalry. Her lover, Li Matin had called him. That was not true. But if he had said the *man she loved*, that might have been true . . . if there had been the chance, she might indeed have loved Rick Morrell.

"Rick," she whispered his name. "Rick . . . "

And all through that lonely, sinister night she stayed there crouched on her knees beside the divan, thinking about him, praying, wondering if either of them would ever see England or home again.

9

THE one week that Li Matin had
given Gay was drawing to an end.
There were only two days left.

In her luxurious prison Gay went nearly
mad. She saw nobody but Li Matin when
he came to visit her and enlarge on the
subject of their future life together. She
did not know what fate had befallen
Rick, and was not likely to know. Li
Matin refused to answer questions, and
appeared angry when she mentioned the
name of the Englishman.

Rick Morrell, however, was by no
means dead. He had at first been
flung into a filthy and indescribable
prison, and then taken with a crowd
of miserable slaves on to the land, those
cruel, sun-baked acres that Li Matin was
attempting to irrigate and fertilize, just
outside Quoon.

Stripped to the waist, wearing only a
loincloth and straw hat, like the natives,
Rick worked . . . till the sweat ran down

126

his body and his muscles ached and his brain seemed numb with the horror of it.

Despite all that he had been drinking lately, he was hard. If he had been less so he would have died. But he managed to stand the physical torture of the slavery, the poor food, and the long hours, and survived. And incidentally he grew fitter every day, until there was not an ounce of superfluous fat on his fine, lithe body, and his mind grew clear and alert, as it had been when he was a boy at Oxford.

The hardest thing of all to endure was the thought of that girl shut up in Li Matin's exotic house. Day after day, night after night, he brooded over the thought of his own escape, and of her rescue.

But unless she managed something, there seemed no way out for him. For he sweated in the fields all day under the vigilant eye of coolie guards, and by night was shut in a small hut with barred windows, and so far he had not succeeded in being able to break open the door or pull down those bars.

It seemed a hopeless affair . . .

And then to Quoon came visitors . . . a high-caste Chinese gentleman and a little lady in satin trousers and tunic, presumably his wife.

Quoon had no objection to visitors. Li Matin welcomed them if they spent money in his bazaar. These visitors took rooms in the rest-house and seemed lavish with their gold.

If they were mysterious and secret in their movements and their speech, who was to know or care? Quoon was full of intrigue and mystery.

But if anyone had looked very closely — which they were given no chance to do — at the face of the little lady under her silken sunshade, they would have seen that her eyes were blue, and her hair red and her skin as white as milk, and realized that she was not Chinese at all.

Lydia Milcroft had come to Quoon.

Part Two

Part Two

10

ANOTHER twenty-four hours passed.

How short a time for those who are happy! How agonizingly long — how seemingly interminable — for those who suffer and are in the depths of despair!

To Gay Burnett, poor little film actress of a disbanded company, that day and night in her gilded prison was as a century. She passed from one stage of suspense and anguish to another. For every hour brought her nearer the end of the week when she must, inevitably, belong to her gaoler. She saw no hope of escape. She was appalled at the prospect of being forced into marriage with the Chinaman. She would have been more resigned to the anticipation of death. But even that solace was denied her, and she realized that it can be more horrible to live than to die.

Not only did her thoughts dwell on her own frightful fate. She thought incessantly of Rick. Rick, who, through her, was also suffering. Forced to live the life of a Chinese slave. What hope was there for him — for either of them?

Since this morning Gay had been allowed out of her gorgeous room. She had found its sinister beauty so oppressive she was thankful to escape from it. She was permitted to sit on the garden terrace of Li Matin's palatial dwelling; an exquisite, artificial garden overlooking the highway into Quoon.

For hours, in solitude, yet knowing herself guarded by slit-like eyes, watching her mysteriously, holding her by silken, invisible chains, Gay sat staring at Quoon with dull brooding gaze.

A silken canopy shielded her from the burning sunlight. A crystal fountain played musically close by, falling in diamond sprays into a marble pool full of swift-moving iridescent fish. Everywhere about her there were tiny trees, dwarf bushes, hundreds of years old; great snow-white flowers and trailing golden mimosa, purple flowers, nameless, and exotic. Little birds with brilliant plumage flew from one branch to another. There were a hundred exquisite, artistic things to look at, to afford pleasure to a lover of beauty and art.

Gay, as lovely and as white as those pale moon-blossoms about her, and with bitterness in her heart, was blind to all the beauty. She loathed it. Her eyes strained towards the distant hills, the desert wastes — towards freedom — the old normal, natural life that lay beyond Quoon.

If only she could find herself free once more; in England, and Rick with her! Yes, she wanted Rick with her. A strange warm love had burst into flower in her aching heart, love for him. She had felt it when she had stood in the circle of his arms for that brief moment yesterday, before Li Matin had found them.

"My dear . . . forgive me . . . " he had whispered against her hair.

The hot tears dripped down her cheeks as she remembered, blotting out the sunlit vision of Quoon and the fantastically lovely terrace-garden on which she was sitting.

"Oh, Rick," she sighed his name aloud, "Rick, I could forgive you anything — if only I thought you loved me."

Now and then she tried to swing a mind half-crazed by terror and grief back to normal things, to old memories. Memories which would help to keep her sane. She was afraid that very soon, if this nightmare went on, she would indeed lose her reason altogether.

She forced herself to remember the Cotswold hills with the snow on them. the vicarage garden, wild and wet in November rain, but hot and sweet-scented with wild thyme and roses in the summer. Her mother — a distant lovely shadow — the photograph of her father in uniform, taken before he was killed in the Great War. Her life with Cousin Gladys in London, and her first introduction to the world of stage and film.

Kind, generous Cousin Gladys. After-noons of shopping. Bargains in sales in Oxford Street, tea in a Lyons Corner House, a 'flick' or a seat at a new show. Cousin Gladys could always wangle a good seat. Week-ends in the country with some of Gladys's friends. A run down to Marlow in the car — tea on the lawn at the 'Compleat Angler'. The cool river and drifting punt. The lilt of a gramophone playing a sentimental record. The soft English twilight, and the smell of night-scented stock, of toasting muffins — of China tea . . .

That last word rambling through Gay's mind pulled her ferociously back to the grim reality of her present fate. The kindly memories of good times in England faded. China! Dear God, here she was in Li Matin's clutches in the heart of Darkest Africa. She wondered chaotically what Cousin Gladys would have thought about it all.

"My dear!" she would have said. "My dear, it isn't true. It couldn't be!"

That was what anyone in England might say. That it *couldn't* be true.

Yet it was, and with a vengeance.

Then suddenly dreams, visions of England, faded and terrible reality struck Gay Burnett again. She sprang to her feet, and pressed her hands to her breast. She stared with rigid eyes at the road below the terrace. She saw a band of men trailing through the dust and heat, a miserable band of slaves, bronzed, half-naked, chained passing dejectedly through

Quoon. They were on their way from the rice-fields to their dwellings. *And Rick Morrell was amongst them!*

Gay saw him. With a wild thrill of horror and pity and compassion, saw the familiar figure of the English trader stumbling along as though half dead with weariness. So tall he was, so perfectly built, that fine brown body. Glistening with sweat, marred with weals where the slave-driver's whip had caught him. She caught her lips between her teeth to stop herself from crying out aloud as she saw those cruel marks. Oh, Rick, poor Rick!

The little band of slaves drew nearer, so near that she could stoop down and speak to them.

She had a passionate wish to attract Rick's attention and say a few words to him. An intense desire for contract with one of her own nationality. Her heart began to pound and the blood rushed to her white cheeks. If she could make Rick see her — speak to him for just one instant . . .

The chance was given to her. For just as Rick came within a few yards of her, the man in front of him — a native from the Cape — collapsed, and with one deep moan lay still in the dust. His endurance was at an end. The guards came up, angry at the delay — cursing. Gay, with dilated eyes, watched them try to revive the wretched man by cruellest methods. But as he gave no sign of returning consciousness they were forced to make an improvised litter and get two of the others to carry him.

This delay gave Gay the opportunity she wanted. Frantically she leaned down from the terrace and called to Rick. He looked up eagerly, saw her and answered. A light flashed into his eyes which were sunk deep in his head and which had been dull and despairing.

"Gay . . . you . . . God! Oh, my dear . . . how are you?"

"Oh, Rick — how are *you*?" she echoed.

"Still alive," he said with a ghost of a smile. "but one might as well be dead."

"I wish I *were* dead!" she said, a sob tearing her throat. "Rick — if only we were together, it could be easier."

"Yes. It wouldn't be quite so hellish

if we could talk occasionally, would it?" he said.

He drew nearer her. The guards were still busy with the wretched Cape black, who was dying. For a moment Rick and Gay saw nothing and nobody in the world but each other. He looked up and thought that she was the loveliest vision he had ever seen. She excluded all memories of Lydia. She was like a lily bent down by the weight of her heavy embroidered Chinese robes. Her limpid blue eyes were too big for her small face and sunken with suffering. He thought: "This girl is good. Money doesn't matter to her. I have been wrong to class her with Lydia. If only I could save her . . . !"

Gay stared down at his exhausted face. Passionate pity for him ached through her very being. She said, huskily:

"Rick, Rick . . . is there no hope of escape for us?"

Before he could answer, she felt a hand touch her hair. Nervous, startled, she swung round. Her heart beat violently. Li Matin had come up behind her. He was tall and stately in his magnificent

Mandarin's robes of jade and gold. He gave her a glittering smile. Hands in his wide sleeves, he bowed low.

"English Rose — I have a visitor to whom I would introduce you. Come . . . !"

He glanced over the terrace and saw the Englishman amongst the other slaves . . . Rick was staring up at them with a grim, tormented face. Li Matin smiled and turned his back.

"Such unpleasant sights are not fitting for the beautiful eyes of my Pearl," he murmured smoothly, and taking Gay's arm, he led her away into the house.

She went with him, hopelessly. Rick, with the other slaves, marched on through the cruel sunlight . . . and was gone.

In one of Li Matin's cool and exquisite rooms, a Chinese lady with a male companion in Mandarin's robes, were taking a refreshing cup of tea with the wealthy ruler of Quoon.

"A friend from Shanghai and his wife," Li Matin told Gay. "I have told them of the lovely English rose who is to be my bride — tomorrow!"

With pride, Li Matin introduced Gay to his friends. She, shuddered and chilled, did not respond to the greeting of Li Matin's visitors. She could think of nothing, nobody but Rick out there in the slaves' compound. Then, as she looked at the woman, her heart seemed to stand still. This was no Chinese lady. She was European. That white and pink skin . . . those big round blue eyes . . . yes, and the red-gold hair under the jewelled scarf . . .

Fresh hope, mingled with fresh doubts and fears, surged into Gay's heart. For now she recognized Mrs. Milcroft. So Lydia was here, in Quoon, posing as a Mandarin's wife. Had she come to help, or to do her more harm? Oh, God, surely even Lydia Milcroft would not stand by and see another English girl forced into the arms of a yellow devil! Yet . . . hope faded again when Gay recalled the fact that it was Lydia who had first tricked and betrayed her to Manuel, and who would, could she have done it, delivered her into Kurt Mulheim's hands.

The two girls looked at each other. But Lydia's eyes, fixed upon Gay, held no pity. For Lydia, not for the first time today, had seen Rick pass through Quoon in the slave-gang. It was Rick upon whom she concentrated. Rick whom she wanted, and she meant to get him. To get him away from Quoon. Gay could stay here, for all Lydia cared — stay here and die. But Lydia had plans more subtle, more cunning than any she had conceived before.

No chance was given to Gay to exchange a single word with Lydia, for as soon as the introductions were made, Gay was taken back to her own room and shut in there. But Li Matin remained to take refreshments with his guests.

Lydia talked in her brightest and best vein to Li Matin. And for once in his life, that wily Chinaman was, himself, deceived. He fully believed that this couple were genuine. For had he not known Ho Kuang in China? It was not difficult to credit what he had been told; that Ho Kuang had married an American lady, a widow with much money. Did he, Li Matin, not intend to do likewise? Li Matin suspected no treachery.

In actual fact, Lydia was neither married to Ho Kuang nor likely to be. When she learned from Mulheim that Manuel had double-crossed him and sold Gay in the slave market at Ligati, Lydia had made further enquiries. It was so easy when one was rich and lavish with bribes. She discovered that Rick Morrell had followed Gay and gone to her rescue, and that he himself had fallen into the hands of the powerful ruler of Quoon.

Lydia was a woman of resource. Her former penchant for Rick — stronger now than ever, because he no longer wanted her — urged her on. She was going to find Rick and win him back. She would be his saviour; he would be grateful. Gay would fade out of the scene, and Rick would soon turn completely to her, Lydia. Such were her plans.

Dollar bills can achieve much. Ho Kuang had been staying in Lydia's hotel. He was in need of money. He had lost a great deal gambling. Lydia approached him, told him her story and offered him a substantial sum to take her to Quoon, pass her off as his wife, and help her rescue her English lover. Ho Kuang — more interested in gold than women — eagerly fell in with her plans.

And Lydia risked nothing by coming here with him. She had left word with the American Consulate where to look for her if she did not return. And Ho Kuang knew it.

The two Chinese, conversing, exchanging the usual bland flattery, were on good terms. Li Matin was led to believe that Kuang had means these days. Anxious to prove himself a generous host, Li Matin turned to Kuang's 'wife' and asked her to name anything that she cared to choose from his treasure as a present to commemorate her visit to Quoon.

"Anything that you ask," he said, bowing low.

Lydia's hard blue eyes narrowed. Her red lips smiled. She said softly:

"Have you not an English slave, Li Matin — a tall and handsome fellow with light grey eyes and curling hair?"

Li Matin bowed.

"That is so."

"Then I ask for him, Li Matin," said Lydia. "I would appreciate his services as a — memento of Quoon."

Li Matin put his tongue in his cheek.

"A curious request," he said unsmilingly.

"No, not so," said Lydia, although every nerve in her body was jumping. "I would like that Englishman as my slave. Years ago, such a man wronged a girl in my house, a young girl of my own blood. I have long wanted my revenge."

Li Matin understood this kind of talk. He, too, would want revenge for such an indignity. He thought he knew what was at the back of the mind of Kuang's 'wife'. She would take the Englishman as her slave and make him pay for his crime against her kinswoman.

After a pause he spoke.

"I had thought to put the Englishman to death, but since you want him, honoured lady, he shall be given to you."

Lydia's heart beat high with triumph. She exchanged glances with Kuang. And Ho Kuang was satisfied. The peculiar American lady had got what she came to Quoon to find. That meant that he, when they returned home, would be well rewarded. Many dollars would be given to him. All was well.

Li Matin clapped his hands. He gave an order to his servants.

"The English slave, bought at Ligati, is to be removed to the honoured dwelling of Ho Kuang, to await the pleasure of the august lady, his wife."

Thus, Rick — the most astonished man in Quoon — found himself taken from his filthy prison and, escorted by two guards, was brought to Li Matin's palace. There he was given a bath and clean white garments, and locked in an ante-room in that part of the building which had been assigned to Li Matin's guests. For Lydia and Kuang had left the rest-house and accepted Li Matin's hospitality for a few days.

Rick — unutterably thankful for the bath, the clean clothes and a plate of food such as he had not tasted for days — was left to himself for an hour to wonder why this change had taken place, and what fate was to befall him next. He feared a trap — treachery of some sort. He could see no reason why Li Matin should show him this kindness, unless Gay had achieved it.

He was dumbfounded when a 'Chinese lady' in embroidered satin robes, entered the ante-room and revealed a familiar pointed little face, crowned with red-gold hair. She looked at him with shining blue eyes, and spoke his name in her well-known voice — clear and high as a peal of bells.

"*Lydia!*" he cried. "Lydia — my God!" And he put a hand to his temples and stared — wondering if he were light-headed — if he had gone mad with suffering, and that this vision of his former lover was a hallucination.

But Lydia soon convinced him that he was neither mad nor dreaming.

"Dearest Rick — thank God my plans have succeeded," she said, and flung herself into his arms.

Mechanically he held her, too dazed to do anything else. It was not because he felt any of the old passion stir in him. His love for Lydia had died . . . been stamped out long ago, when she had annihilated his faith in womankind. But he was mad with joy and hope and gratitude when he realized that she had come to Quoon to save him.

She told him a wonderful story, only half-true. He was not in the state of mind to take it in very clearly. He was given to understand, anyhow, that Lydia had come from Chicago to West Africa to find him. When she called at his bungalow and found him gone, and later met Mulheim and heard of Gay's disappearance, she had traced them to Ligati and from Ligati to Quoon, with the help of Ho Kuang.

"Now that Li Matin has given you to me as my slave, all will be easy," Lydia told him. "We can make our plans to leave Quoon together."

"What plans?"

She drew a case from her bag and handed it to him. He took the Virginia cigarette, and she lighted it for him and noted how his hand trembled, and how grey and gaunt his face was under the tan. She realized what he must have suffered. She pitied him vaguely, but thought the whole thing the most thrilling adventure of her life, and the very fact that it was so bizarre, so sensational, appealed to her because she was so much a sensationalist herself.

He looked at the cigarette, drew a deep breath of it and said:

"God, that's good!"

147

She put her hand on his arm.

"Sit down, poor Ricky . . . "

He flushed and turned his attention to her, becoming more conscious every moment of the fact that this *was* Lydia, this little piece of porcelain who might have stepped out of a Chinese picture, so dainty, so fair, so exquisitely made-up was she as a high-caste Chinese lady. Drunk, not with wine, but with the joy of the first cigarette which he had smoked for days, the first good meal he had tasted, the first real glimpse of rescue, he laughed aloud.

"Princess Precious Steam!" he exclaimed. "Wasn't there a play called that running in London once? Didn't we see it together? You look as though you were an advertisement for her."

"We saw many things together, Ricky, didn't we?" she answered.

Her old pet name for him woke memories that were as bitter as they were sweet. How he had loved this woman! How he had hated her, too, after she had shattered his faith and rejected his love. He rubbed his hand across his forehead in a bewildered way.

"Lydia," he said, "the whole of this business doesn't seem at all real to me. It might be a piece of damn-fool film or a cheap thriller. But don't tell me that I, Richard Morrell, have been sold to you, Lydia, as a *slave!*"

He finished on a laugh that cracked, and added:

"No, I think I'll wake up in a moment and find myself back in the hotel, in the car, drinking myself to death."

She bit her lip.

"That's why I came all the way from America, Ricky," she said softly, "to stop you from doing that any more."

"Why?" he asked bluntly. "What the devil can it matter to you what happened to me? You walked out on me. The day before our wedding . . . the day of my mother's death. You didn't care then whether I lived or died."

"I did," she said. "Only there are reasons . . . I haven't time to explain them . . . why I had to accept Roger and go to America. If you think I didn't suffer too, if you think I stopped loving you, you're wrong."

His lips twisted.

"No, Lydia, I'm not swallowing that. I believed in you once, but I am not going to believe in you again."

She was suddenly irritated. She wanted Rick to walk straight back into her arms without too much fuss or trouble. Since she had seen him last, she had been bored to death by the advances of a senile old idiot who had only made it worth her while to leave Rick because of the wealth behind a Chicago millionaire. She had been showered with money. Her diamonds, her emeralds, were bigger than the jewels of any other woman in Chicago. Her word had been law. She had what she had always played for since she was a young girl . . . the possession of beauty and money combined. But there was one thing which she knew that money could not buy. That was the love of a man like Rick Morrell. She had never known another love like his. She had remembered it with unceasing regret once the Atlantic had separated them. Then Roger's death, leaving her free with his dollars behind her, had seemed a grand opportunity to get back what she had flung away. The old thrilling adoration from Rick. He had always been able to stir her blood. She knew that he stirred it now. He was more than ever interesting with that deeply lined face which had been burnt so dark brown in the rice-fields.

She said:

"Don't think too much about anything, Ricky. Let it slide. Just know that I've come to save you. That's why I'm here, and whatever I've done in the past to you, you can trust me now."

Suddenly he remembered Gay Burnett. He was shocked with himself for having forgotten her for the moment in the astonishment of this reunion — if it could be called that — with Lydia. And remembering her as he had last seen her, so white, so haunted by terror, he became conscious of the salient fact that he cared more what happened to her than what happened to himself. And she mattered to him more than Lydia. (Lydia could never really matter again.)

He said:

"You know, of course, that the little English film actress, Gay Burnett, is also Li Matin's prisoner?"

"Yes, I've seen her."

"Well, of course, we must take her with us. We must save her. That yellow fiend is trying to induce her to go through a form of marriage with him. We can't allow that. I know you'll agree."

Lydia looked through her long lashes. She hated the very sound of Gay's name. She was bitterly angry because Rick's first thought was for Gay. Nevertheless, she had taken it for granted that she must include Gay in the escape, otherwise it would put Rick against her. It would seem too utterly callous. Yes, let Gay escape with them . . . from this place, but from Quoon, *with Rick* — never. Lydia had other plans . . .

She smiled up at her former lover.

"Of course we will save this girl," she said.

"Lydia — I'm deeply grateful! My God — what a lot we shall owe you!" he said hoarsely. He felt half crazy at the thought of freedom after the days of torture through which he and Gay had passed. He even began to wonder if he had misjudged Lydia. She must have cared for him a little to come all these thousands of miles to make contact with him again.

Then Lydia's subtle voice said:

"Mind you, it is for her own sake she must be saved, but I am not sure — "

"What?"

"That she would really thank me."

"Don't be ridiculous. The child is demented with terror."

Lydia shrugged her shoulders.

"Ho Kuang has heard that Gay is not so indifferent to the advances of the great Li Matin. After all, the wealth and luxury of her position may attract a penniless out-of-work walk-on."

Rick was silent for a moment. Then he gave a short laugh.

"That, of course, is rot," he said. "Now let's make plans, Lydia . . . "

But she wondered if she had planted just the tiniest seed of doubt about Gay in his mind. She hoped at least that he would remember what she had said about Gay.

11

NIGHT had fallen over Quoon. In
her beautiful room — suffocatingly
hot and over-scented — Gay
trailed up and down in her long,
silken robe, wondering how she could
put an end to her life before dawn
came, and Li Matin should force her
to the wedding ceremony. Round and
round in her mind circled the thought of
Rick . . . Rick, whom she imagined to be
still a member of that terrible slave-gang.
If only he could be spared, she thought.
What could she do to help him? Putting
aside her own suffering, her heart ached
at the memory of Rick's exhausted face.
It was obvious that it would not be
long before his resistance snapped and
he would follow the Cape coolie who
had died of over-strained heart.

An evening meal — exquisitely cooked
and served — little Oriental dishes of tiny
birds, vegetables and sweet-meats — was
brought to Gay. She ate very little. Tears

154

of sheer loneliness rolled slowly down her cheeks as she sat there. When she had finished, Li Matin paid her the usual ceremonial visit. He was gorgeous in black and silver robes. His aristocratic face was bland, as inscrutable as usual. She shrank from him as he took her hand in greeting. He made a gesture of regret as he saw her move away.

"So you still have no love in your heart for me, English Rose?" he murmured. "Alas! Must I take an unwilling bride in my embrace tomorrow?"

Gay stared at him wild-eyed. Then she thought:

"If I *pretend* to like him — to be more willing — would he do something, anything, for me? *Would he let Rick go free?*"

A wild forlorn hope, but it was worth risking, worth a sacrifice. For if she must be sacrificed to Li Matin anyhow, why not make use of it? She steeled herself to remember that she had once been an actress. She must act now for Rick's sake. He had come here to try to save her. It was up to her now to rescue him from a dreadful death, if she could.

She managed a smile to the Chinaman. The first smile he had ever received from her, and it enchanted him.

"Perhaps I am not so — reluctant — after all," she said, her lips dry, the palms of her hands wet.

Li Matin's almond eyes glittered. He drew nearer to her.

"White Rose — Pearl of the West — if you could learn to love me as I love you — the whole of Quoon shall be yours, and all that's in it!" he said with sudden passion.

She felt sick and more afraid than she had ever been in her whole life. She wondered how to bear it. But his words gave her courage. 'Quoon and all that was in it'. Rick was in Quoon. He must give her Rick's life — in return for her embraces . . .

She forced herself to smile at him again.

"I think I could love you," she said, coldly and clearly, "if you would really give me anything in your possession that I wanted."

"Anything!" he repeated eagerly. "Anything . . . "

And he lifted both her hands and put them against his forehead in homage. She stood suffering it, trying to pluck up the courage to ask him for Rick's release.

Through a fine transparent screen a man passed and heard these words.

It was Rick Morrell. Rick with the keys of the palace in his hand. Rick, knowing that through the successful efforts of Ho Kuang and Lydia, every guard in the palace had been doped with drugged wine and could offer no resistance.

He had not come in time to hear Gay's original appeal for mercy. He knew only that she was giving Li Matin a promise of love in return for what he might offer her. He was filled with a sense of acute disappointment in her. It seemed possible now that Lydia's insinuations had truth in them. Perhaps Gay, the poor little film actress, *was* attracted by the thought of Li Matin's wealth, and growing more resigned to her fate at his hands. God! Didn't he know the power that money had over women? Wasn't that how he had lost Lydia? Well, he wasn't going to break his heart about it, but he was going to take Gay Burnett away, that was the

157

one clear thought in his head. Whether she was becoming attached to her gilded prison or not, he was going to remove her from it.

He was strong . . . strong with the good food and wine which he had been given, and with the knowledge that he had it within his power to escape. He did not wait to hear any more between these two. He went straight through that screen, splitting it from top to bottom.

There was a scream from Gay, followed by an astonished and joyful cry:

"Rick!"

He had no time for her then. He hurled himself upon the Chinaman. A look of consternation wiped the blandness from that yellow face just for an instant. Then Rick's strong brown fingers were at his throat, and with a gurgling sound the Mandarin dropped in a heap on the ground.

Rick wiped his hands.

"Grand! I've been longing to do that for days."

Gay looked up at him in bewilderment.

"How did you dare? Where are the guards"

158

"They're asleep and I'm in the mood to dare to do anything," he said. "You're coming with me whether you want to or not."

"But of course I want to. Heavens, what do you think . . . "

"I haven't time to think now. All I know is that we both of us owe our lives to Lydia Milcroft. She and Kuang are at the House of the Seven Dragons. We are all of us leaving Quoon for good."

She could not understand why he spoke to her as though she was reluctant to go. There seemed little of friendliness in his manner. But nothing much mattered except that she saw a light in the darkness at last, and knew that by some miracle she and Rick were going to be free again.

She went with him without a word. He guided her out of the palace on to the starlit terrace. Once or twice she stumbled over her long robe and he caught her arm and saved her from falling. He took great strides and she found it difficult to keep up with him. He seemed to know his way and she asked no questions. To leave that dreadful palace behind her was such a relief that

159

no words could have expressed it.

They came to a house built in pagoda style and with the sign of a Dragon over the door. "The House of the Seven Dragons" was Quoon's apology for an hotel. A den of gambling and dancing and a rendezvous for the backwash of darkest Africa.

Rick had his instructions from Ho Kuang. He knocked three times on the door, which opened automatically. He pushed Gay Burnett in front of him. Once they were inside he would talk to her, and demand an explanation for those inexplicable words which he had heard her saying to Li Matin. Damn it, he didn't want to be fond of her, but he was fond of her against his will. There was something so brave about her. Something that drew her to him against his will and made even more the focus of his interest than Lydia, who had rescued him from the hell in Li Matin's slave gang.

Then, before he could think, the lights inside the rest-house went out. He was jostled away from Gay. He felt many hands, heard many voices speaking in many native languages. He called out:

"Gay! Gay!"

He heard a cry in the distance:

"Oh, Rick . . . Rick, where are you?"

He began to strike out with his fists, his teeth clenched.

"What the hell . . . put on some light . . . "

And then the lights went up. And he found himself in a room with only two people in it. Lydia Milcroft and Kuang, her ally.

12

GAY screamed in vain as she felt a pair of sinewy arms pick her up in that sudden darkness and lift her off her feet. She struggled furiously, aware that she was in fresh danger. Then she was set on her feet again. Lights flashed on. She stared dazedly about her. She found herself in a small room, furnished in Oriental style, face to face with her former employer, Kurt Mulheim.

Her astonishment was so great that she could only blink at him stupidly. Mulheim, just the same as ever. Blond, plump, eyes smiling behind the powerful lenses of his glasses, white suit immaculate. Mulheim — in *Quoon*! Gay could not gather her scattered thoughts. Speechlessly, she looked at him. He bowed.

"Why, if it is not my little Gay! Life is indeed full of happy surprises, *gnädige Fräulein* . . . "

And he thought how remarkably astute

Lydia Milcroft had been. Once she had traced Gay to Quoon, she had sent word to him by a native runner. He had come in hot haste. He wanted Gay as he had never wanted any woman in his life. Twice she had escaped him. The last time when Manuel, the traitor, had double-crossed him. But this time she would not escape.

Then a cry broke from Gay's lips.

"This is another trap — that woman, Lydia Milcroft, has done it — oh, my God — if Rick knew!"

Her voice rose to a frienzied shriek and she turned to run, but Mulheim caught her wrists.

"Little fool — these walls are padded and nobody takes any notice of screams in the House of the Seven Dragons. Be quiet. I am not Manuel. I am a civilized German. I shall not sell you in the slave market. I'm going to take you away from Quoon. I shall take you immediately back and then on to Johannesburg, where we shall get married at last, *hein*?"

"Rick!" she repeated frantically.

"What is the use of calling on him? He brought you here to me."

"No — no — that's a lie!" she gasped.

"It's true, I tell you. He and Mrs. Milcroft planned the whole thing. Don't you know that they were once engaged to be married and will be again? Those two are responsible for my being here! They wanted to get rid of you. They sent for me."

She stared at him. She felt sick to the very soul. She knew perfectly well that Rick would never have betrayed her into Mulheim's hands. She knew that Lydia, alone, was responsible. The disappointment of finding herself again a captive overwhelmed her.

She felt defeated. She covered her face with her hands.

"Oh God, help me!"

"No — I'll help you — so long as you do what I tell you." said Mulheim with his familiar guttural laugh. "Come — pull yourself together, *Liebchen*. You cannot object to me as strenuously as you did to the venerable Mandarin."

"I don't," she said, with a hopeless laugh. "But to be quite candid, I don't care for either of you."

"What a little fool you are! I have

much more to offer you than you realize. My film company was . . . what you call in England . . . a blind, *hein*? My American nationality . . . that, too, is a trick. You see, Gay, I am really a good German. I work for the leaders of the great Nazi movement. It is not only in Europe that we need allies. It is out here. Also in India, in Malaya, in China. All over the world the Feuhrer has placed his mark and I'm helping to put it there."

She hardly heard what he was saying. She dropped limply into a chair.

"I go from one horror to another," she said.

He stood before her, scowling.

"You do not know the meaning of the word 'horror'."

She raised a little white face to his.

"Can you imagine what it was like in that outrageous slave market? As a film director, you should know . . . " She laughed, her voice cracking.

"Ah, I know you have been through much. But there are worse horrors waiting for the enemies of my Government. Are you so unconcerned with politics, my little one?"

"Yes," she said blandly. "I'm unconcerned with everything except leaving Quoon."

He ignored this and began to walk up and down the little room, talking, half to her, half to himself, the look of a fanatic on his face.

"I see a new Germany to which your England shall be subordinate. I see a new Government here and in all parts of the world. And it shall be *my* Government. I see you as my wife. Nobody shall object to that English blood which is in you, because you, as my wife, shall take my nationality. With your beauty, your charm, and your command of the language, you shall help me in my work. We shall go back to Europe together. There is much there to be done, and — "

"Oh, be quiet!" she interrupted with a sudden wail. "Do stop all this talking, and tell me that you'll take me home."

He looked at her, his eyes pin-points behind the thick glasses.

"Home with me, yes, if you wish it."

"Very well," she said with a gesture of despair, "home with you."

13

RICK MORRELL was going through a bad half-hour.

When he had first been confronted by Lydia and Kuang, her Chinese ally, he had immediately asked them to assist him in search for Gay.

"She was with me up to a moment ago," he said hoarsely. "Then as soon as we got inside this infernal place she was deliberately jostled away from me in the darkness. Spirited away by some fiend. She's got to be found, I tell you. She's been through enough, that poor child. Enough to send her raving mad."

Lydia looked at Ho Kuang. She assumed an expression of complete innocence.

"I haven't the least idea what can have happened to Miss Burnett. Go, Kuang, and make immediate enquiries."

Alone with Lydia, Rick looked at her with bloodshot eyes.

"You've helped us escape from that

yellow devil's palace, but it's not going to be much good to me if I get away and that poor kid doesn't."

His words struck unpleasantly upon Lydia's ears. Rick was far too interested in Gay Burnett. But she spoke with that sweetness which she could muster at will.

"Poor Rick! Naturally you don't want to go away without her. And no doubt she will be found. Kuang will find her. At the same time, I have no reason to suppose that she has been, as you call it, spirited away. The House of the Seven Dragons is a public place. No one would stop her finding you if she wished to."

"That's ridiculous," said Rick tersely. "The whole place is a nightmare and full of monstrous people. No white girl is safe here for a single minute."

Said Lydia:

"What does this girl mean to you, Rick?"

He sat down, suddenly tired and unnerved by his recent ordeal. He ran his fingers through his hair.

"I don't know. I'm not sure. There's something about her that appeals to me very deeply. We've been through a good bit together. But whatever I feel for her, I've got to save her from this place."

"I see," said Lydia, and then added: "I seem to have come a good many thousand miles for nothing."

He looked up at her warily.

"I don't really know why you did come."

"I don't think this is the time or place to discuss it," she said, with a slow, strange smile. "I only know that I don't want you to be unhappy any more, Rick. I feel guilty enough as it is for all that you've been through — through me. I came here from America to tell you that, and to ask for your forgiveness."

He nodded and sighed deeply. He felt stupid with fatigue, with the conflict of feelings which he had been through so recently. At times, during his imprisonment with Li Matin's slaves, he had wondered whether he was already mad and suffering from a succession of frightful nightmares. Or whether it was the result of drink. A kind of delirum-tremens. One thing only seemed clear to him: that he would never again be the Rick Morrell who had come out to Africa and started to degenerate so shamefully. The damn-fool drunkard whom Gay Burnett had first met, and to whom she had appealed for help, was a creature of the past. He blamed himself for so much that had happened to Gay. If he had been sober and in his right mind that night, he would never have insulted her, left her alone in the bungalow and driven her away — to this!

He wished he did not feel so damnably ill. There was a stinging pain in his temples and when he lifted his head he was gripped by a feeling of acute nausea.

He hardly heard what Lydia had to say. That clear, tinkling voice of hers which had once given him so much joy, so much satisfaction in life, had no particular effect upon him. Lydia herself was curiously ineffective now, he thought. It was Gay — little Gay Burnett — whom he wanted. Gay, whom he had, for a moment, held in his arms. Gay, with her warm friendly smile, her sense of good comradeship, her amazing courage in the face of the horrors through which she had passed.

Ho Kuang returned. He had had his orders from Lydia and he knew what to say.

He regretted, he declared, that he could not bring the other English lady to the honourable gentleman, because she had already left the House of the Seven Dragons.

Rick sprang to his feet and stood rocking there a little.

"Left — with whom? *What the hell* . . . ?" He began to shout.

Lydia's hand restrained him.

"Quiet, Rick. Leave this to me."

She questioned Ho Kuang, who put the answers exactly as he had been instructed. Lydia assumed a state of perplexity.

"The mystery deepens. Kuang says that Gay went away with a European, not a native. A plump man with glasses who spoke with a strong German accent."

Rick drew a hand across his eyes. He wished he could think clearly. But he was neither physically nor mentally fit to cope with the facts of Gay's disappearance. However, he could not fail to draw one conclusion from Lydia's words.

171

"But good God! That sounds like Mulheim."

"It obviously *is* Mulheim," she said.

"But what was he doing here?"

"He came to Quoon for her, perhaps."

"But she loathed the man. She was terrified of him. She would *never* go away alone with him."

Lydia smiled.

"I think, Rick, you're a little impulsive. Gay Burnett is really a stranger to you. You know nothing about her. It is quite likely she is more interested in this man than you think. He was the lead of her film company. Didn't you tell me that he wished to marry her? Maybe she has chosen to go back to civilization with him."

Rick stood hesitant. He was torn between doubts and fears. And he was conscious of a very real disappointment that Gay could not be found. He wanted her with him. He wanted, personally, to make sure that she was all right. This story about Mulheim's presence in Quoon was unbelievable. But the whole sequence of events these last few days had been so fantastic that he realized that anything might be true.

"We must make another search for her," he said thickly.

Lydia set her teeth. This stubborn desire on Rick's part to make contact with Gay did not at all fit with her particular schemes.

She said:

"You're being foolish, Rick. You must remember that your own life is in danger — and Kuang's and mine. You seem to be thinking only of this Burnett girl. But what about me and my safety?"

"I want you to be safe, too," he muttered.

The pain in his head was growing worse. The hot room, full of the sickly smell of burning joss-sticks, was overpowering him, and Lydia watched him, knowing that he was ill and waiting for his collapse.

When it came, she acted quickly.

Rick Morrell could neither stand properly nor collect his scattered thoughts when Kuang and the white woman led him out of the House of the Seven Dragons. He babbled about Gay, implored them help him find her, repudiated the story of Mulheim . . . a jumble of words, incoherent and difficult. And Lydia humoured him and tried to quieten him; and at the same time knew that he was incapable of putting up further resistance, so that she could carry out her own plans.

Whatever she knew about Kurt Mulheim and Gay, she was not going to impart to Rick.

So Rick left Quoon that night, quietly and unobtrusively, hitting the desert trail with camels, coolies and the necessary equipment which Lydia had brought to Quoon.

In Li Matin's palace there was chaos. The ruler of Quoon had been discovered, half murdered; his white captives and his Chinese guests had vanished. Li Matin was too ill to give any orders and did nothing. So there was nothing to prevent Rick and his companions from getting away.

Every mile they travelled into the desert away from Quoon, however, Rick's sudden sickness grew worse, but he still, in his conscious moments, worried about

Gay and called for her. He could not stifle his fears that she had been left behind — a white girl, a young and beautiful Englishwoman — in that terrible place. In Quoon — city of iniquity — of vice and cruelty and slavery.

Between bouts of severe fever, Rick brooded and tormented himself with memories of her. Lydia knew what was in his mind and lost no opportunity in poisoning his mind against the girl.

"Don't worry about her — forget her — she isn't in any danger. Mulheim will look after her."

"But where have they gone? How can we be sure she is safe?"

"Ho Kuang is sure of it, Rick — dearest — don't worry. Just try to get well and strong again. I can promise you, you will find that Gay and Mulheim are together."

He looked into her ardent eyes and with a sense of shock knew that Lydia was his for the asking again. Every word, every expression told him so. But it did not thrill him. That kind of feeling for Lydia was dead. He was grateful to her. But if his blood stirred at all it was for

175

Gay Burnett. He could not reconcile himself to the thought that she was with the German.

They travelled all night until they were some distance from Quoon. In the cool of the dawn they dismounted from their camels, set up tents, and rested.

Rick, half delirious, slept heavily under the dope Lydia gave him. But while he slept, a little altercation took place between Mrs. Roger Milcroft and Ho Kuang. Ho Kuang had been instrumental in bringing Lydia to Quoon, in rescuing her Englishman from Li Matin's palace and bringing them safely out of the place again. And he wanted his reward.

Lydia, now that she had gained her purpose, was not so anxious to part with as much money as he suggested as a reward. She told Ho Kuang that he asked too much.

"It is more than I promised," she said.

The Chinaman's eyes became mere slits. He smiled dangerously.

"I think not, honourable lady," he said. "If you will look back, you will remember that you arranged to pay me ten thousand dollars. For less I would not have risked losing my life in Quoon."

Lydia was a clever woman up to a point. Her great failing was meanness, and she could not conquer it now. She was foolish enough to argue with Ho Kuang, believing him to be under her sway.

"You are wrong," she smiled. "It was half that, and you know it."

Silence. Ho Kuang's yellow face did not change expression. He was an Oriental. He continued to smile. But his heart was red-hot with fury and resentment. So the white woman had fooled him and would not pay up? Ho Kuang did not argue. But his vengeance fell upon her swiftly.

He turned and walked from her towards the Englishman's tent. Lydia, believing that he was, as she had expected, a stupid fellow pleased enough with five thousand dollars, forgot him.

But Ho Kuang woke Rick and told him the truth.

Rick listened to a strange story. He could scarcely take it all in. He was half-doped with exhaustion and the fever which had gripped him, suddenly and fiercely. He was shivering with ague while he sat there in his tent, wrapped in Lydia's fur rug, listening to the Chinaman.

"I thought honourable gentleman would like to know," Ho Kuang said smoothly and treacherously. "The English lady with us has betrayed you, and the friend who has been left in Quoon is the victim of her plot."

Rick looked with brilliant, fever-glazed eyes at the Chinaman.

"What the hell do you mean?"

Ho Kuang bowed low.

"It is as I say . . . listen, honourable sir . . ."

And Rick listened, struggling against the fever. He knew that Lydia was even more vile than he had thought her when she had walked out on him. She was doubly a traitor. She had put Gay in the German's power, and was the original cause of Gay's betrayal into Manuel's hand. Through Lydia, the little film actress had been taken to the terrible slave market at Ligati.

Gradually the whole sinister plot was

unfolded to Rick. The revelation of it filled him with horror and astonishment. He had no cause to doubt that Ho Kuang spoke the truth. It was equally apparent that Kuang was for some good reason annoyed with Lydia. But all that concerned Rick was the knowledge that Gay was in Mulheim's hands. And that he, Rick, would not go another step further towards civilization without her.

Head whirling, every limb racked with fever, he stood up and gripped the Chinaman's arms.

"You've said enough, Kuang," he exclaimed hoarsely. "Kuang — listen to me. We must go back to Quoon — at once — and save that girl. Are you game?"

Ho Kuang spread out his hands with an Oriental gesture of fatalism.

"If you go back — it will be certain death — "

"That doesn't matter. What about that poor English lady?"

"It is indeed unfortunate for her," said Kuang.

Blindly, Rick staggered out of the tent. Damn this fever, he thought. His head

179

was spinning round and his legs trembled under him. Through a haze, the small figure of Lydia appeared. Rage choked him. He pointed a finger at her.

"You vile . . . treacherous — "

He stopped and fell at her feet. The fever, the narcotics he had taken, overpowered him. Everything was blacked out, and Lydia went down on her knees beside him. White to the lips, she stared up at Ho Kuang.

"What have you told him, *you* — "

"All!" broke in the Chinaman, smiling. "You have honourable self to thank. You break your word. Ho Kuang breaks his. Honourable gentleman wished to return to Quoon to save the other white lady."

"He never will!" said Lydia between her teeth. With burning eyes she stared down at the man whom she wanted for herself with all the passion of which her shallow nature was capable. "He's very sick. His illness is worse, Kuang. It will be days before he can walk. The coolies must go on carrying him by hammock. But not to Quoon. We go in the opposite direction, Ho Kuang. You are going to help me, and this time I will pay you before we start."

The Chinaman bowed.

"Under those circumstances, honourable lady, I shall do all in my power to assist," he said blandly.

So it was under those circumstances that Rick, semi-conscious, was carried across the desert away from Quoon, beyond Ligati and back to civilization to that coastal town wherein he had first met Gay. He was put to bed in his own bungalow two days later.

There were moments when he grew conscious enough to remember everything that Ho Kuang had told him. Then he raved against Lydia, cursed the pair of them, demanded to be taken back to Quoon. But Lydia, who sat beside him, only smiled and tried to calm him down.

"The fever has turned your brain, Ricky. You are dreaming," she would say in her high, flute-like voice.

But Rick knew that he was not dreaming. He called for Gay, babbled of her; delirious, helpless in the hands of the woman who had deceived and tricked him.

His despair was unlimited when he found himself in his own home and knew that many hundreds of miles lay between him and Quoon. And that little Gay Burnett had been left to her fate at the mercy of the Nazi agent.

14

WHEN Mulheim told Gay that Rick and Lydia had left the House of the Seven Dragons, and that she was alone with him, Gay gave up struggling against the German. She abandoned all hope of finding Rick. She supposed he had abandoned her. Just left Quoon with his former love. She, Gay, was of no consequence.

When she questioned Mulheim, his replies were evasive.

"I cannot tell you much, except that they tell me here that the American lady and the Englishman set forth an hour ago on their return journey to the coast. He is still interested in Mrs. Milcroft. He can mean nothing in your life, *mein Liebchen*."

She looked at her captor dully.

"Something must have happened . . . something must have been said about me . . . to make him think I wasn't worth saving."

Mulheim smiled.

"Not at all. He was told that *I* was here to look after you. He has left you to me."

An instant's silence. Gay winced under that new blow. She sensed further treachery on the part of Lydia Milcroft. She said under her breath:

"So that's it! The fiend of a woman has made him think that I have come willingly to you."

Mulheim took her hand.

"Isn't that true, *Liebchen*? Haven't you just said that you will come with me?"

All powers of resistance seemed to leave her. She said:

"I shan't fight any more. Get me out of here. I keep telling you . . . get me out. Unless you want a crazy idiot on your hands. I can't stand much more."

Mulheim did what she asked. He was, for the moment, kind and considerate. Gay was, in his opinion, beaten and ready to do anything that he asked of her. He had work for her to do in Johannesburg. He would join two other important agents there. There was much

184

to be done in Johannesburg to spread the propaganda for the Fatherland. He lost the desire to hurt or bully Gay. And he was frightened that she might fall ill and die. He did not want that to happen. He wanted this fair young thing as his wife. *Frau Mulheim*. Working for him and with him, for the Fuehrer.

He got her out of the House of the Seven Dragons. He had come in answer to Lydia's message by car to Ligati, and then by camel, with a bodyguard of African coolies, to Quoon. He would take Gay back the same way. At Ligati they would pick up his car and drive comfortably back to civilization. Nobody hindered him when he piloted Gay out of that sinister house of pleasure. Half the inmates were drugged with opium, and with Li Matin lying half-dead in his bed Quoon was in chaos. The guards on the fringe of the city had deserted their posts. Without being hindered or questioned, Mulheim and the girl found their way into the desert and struck the trail that Rick and his companions had hit only a few hours before them.

Gay — like one exhausted in mind

and body — lay unresisting in Mulheim's arms, on his camel. It swayed and jolted. She did not mind. She was too tired to care. Rick had gone from her for ever. Hope was dead. She had only one desire now — to get back to England and never to see Liberia and Africa again.

"You belong to me, *Liebchen*," Mulheim had said when he first lifted her up on to his camel and then set out on that long journey. "You are going to marry me — as soon as we reach Johannesburg."

Gay looked up into the man's plump, eager face. She was almost past caring what happened to her. But not entirely.

"Leave me alone. I don't want to marry anybody." She said dully.

"But you will marry me," he said.

"No," she said wearily, and again, "No!"

"Do you prefer, then, to stay in Quoon, or be sold in Ligati as a slave, *hein*?"

She shuddered.

"No — my God, no!"

"Then you must make your choice," said Mulheim. "Your gallant English friend, Mr. Morrell, has deserted you. No use to hope that he will rescue you."

Gay saw no argument against that. In reality she was not sure whether Rick had deserted her or been lured into another of the infamous Lydia's traps. If only she could see him and tell him that she loved him and had been willing to save him at the expense of herself. If only she could see him and speak to him once again.

Hour after hour, during that journey under the stars, across the African desert, Mulheim persisted in his wooing, as romantically as a German can make love.

"Don't go on fighting against me, my *Liebechen*. Be sensible and marry me. I have never offered marriage to any other woman on earth but you. I swear I'll be good to you. If I've been unkind to you in the past, I'm sorry. You are lovely and good. I know you are good, and I'm crazy about you. I shall make a good German of you and you shall do much for me and my Fuehrer."

She shut her eyes, every fibre of her being shrinking from the man. She was broken and defeated. And she saw no hope, no glimmer of light, in the darkness. What use to battle with this man? He was too powerful for her. Futile to argue or resist. Better to do as he said and give him her promise to marry him. If she refused, if she upset him, he might leave her in Ligati and she would never see England again. She was so tired of the struggle and of suffering. She could not go through the horrors of these last few days again. Like a nightmare, all the terrible memories haunted her. She saw herself once more in the slave market at Ligati, and Li Matin bidding for her. She remembered the magnificence of his gilded palace, and how she had dreaded the day of reckoning with him. She hungered for peace and forgetfulness.

Was there no other way out? She did not want to marry Kurt Mulheim. He was evil and cruel. The devil lay behind those light, short-sighted eyes of his. She had heard stories of Germany, of Nazi agents — the Gestapo. But unless she humoured him and temporized, she might be exposed to worse misery.

When they stopped to give some rest to the caravan, for it was a long and hot and difficult journey to Ligati, Gay bargained with Mulheim as though for her life.

"Leave me alone now — and I will marry you when we get to Johannesburg. I promise," she said.

She made that promise standing before him outside the tent which the coolies had erected for her. She was travel-stained, haggard and thin, but still lovely in her embroidered Chinese robes. In the moonlight her face looked so wan, so ivory white, and her eyes were so sunken that the German was moved, momentarily, to pity.

"You are tired — you shall sleep," he said kindly. "I won't disturb you, *Liebchen*. But understand — when we are at the end of this journey — you will marry me?"

"Yes," she said.

He beamed through his glasses.

"You shall drink a toast to me — and to Germany," he said. "You shall never regret it. I shall love you, Gay. You shall be loved and respected by all in Munich, which is my home."

He left her alone after that, and she knew that she had nothing to fear so long as she kept her promise to marry him. She lay down on the camp-bed, utterly exhausted. Her heart cried out for Rick, and during the days and nights that followed she was tormented with the longing to see him again, to tell him that she cared, to make him understand that she had been forcibly detained by Mulheim, and then when he knew, even if he loved Lydia still, some of this intolerable anguish which was eating her would be cured.

They came to Ligati. Here Mulheim obtained clothes for her in the bazaar. With enormous relief she flung away the hateful Chinese dress, and was once more dressed as a European. There was nothing that could not be bought in the bazaar at Ligati. Everything was stolen property. Mulheim found for her a white riding-shirt, khaki breeches and a sun-helmet. She had grown so thin during her captivity in Quoon that she was like a slim boy in that attire. In the car, driving towards the coast, Mulheim looked at her with a new appreciation. He said:

"No matter what you wear, you are always as lovely as a flower, *Liebchen*.

But you are too pale and slight now. Once you are my wife, my kisses will bring back the roses, *hein*?"

She made no answer, but a slight tremor passed through her. She stared blindly at the fierce, sunlit country through which they were driving, and thought:

"Rick, Rick, every mile is bringing me nearer to you. But what can I do to get away from this man? How shall I see you again and make you understand what I feel for you?"

Her sensations were indescribable when, once more, after the long journey, she found herself in that coastal town from which she had been tricked by Lydia, weeks ago. It seemed to her many years, indeed a lifetime, since she had left it, so crammed with horror had those weeks been.

Kurt Mulheim gave her neither time nor opportunity to escape from him and find her way to Rick's bungalow, if that were her intention. He took her straight to the hotel.

"I will send a man for our tickets. We will leave by train today," he said.

"There is no object in waiting, and we can take the mail train south to Johannesburg."

In despair, Gay went with him to the hotel. It was, in its way, a relief to be back in a civilized town full of white, friendly faces. But the presence of Kurt Mulheim was a constant menace. She was still a slave — his slave. She wondered, desperately, how to escape him, how to find Rick Morrell.

Then, suddenly, as they walked up on to the wide verandah into the hotel, she noticed a woman standing there, a small, familiar figure in a white dress, with a green sunshade over her lovely little red head. *Lydia*. Of course, Lydia was back here again. She had come back with Rick.

Lydia Milcroft saw Gay.

The woman who had been the cause of all her misery paused and looked at the other girl. There was nothing but malice in her cold eyes. So Gay Burnett had got back from Quoon. With the German. If there was anybody on earth whom Lydia disliked, it was Gay. Through Gay, Lydia had lost Rick. Otherwise she would have got him back. She knew it.

Two days ago Rick had recovered from that long bout of fever — the worst he had ever had — and once able to escape from Lydia's vigilant eye had left the bungalow and made immediate arrangements to return to Quoon. And before leaving home he told Lydia what he thought of her. It had not been a particularly pleasant hour for Lydia. Still weak and thin, and far from fit for that long journey, he nevertheless embarked upon it. Gay Burnett had been left in Quoon to the mercy of Mulheim. Rick was going back for her, if he died in the attempt. And this time he was taking a couple of British officers with him. Members of the police who were a little dubious of the trader's fantastic story of the slave market at Ligati, but willing to investigate.

Lydia, thwarted and furious, now centred all her hatred upon Gay Burnett.

"So you've got back, have you? Well — perhaps it will interest you to know that you'll never set eyes on Rick Morrell again." She said.

Gay gave her a bitter look.

193

"I realize I have you to thank for that, Mrs. Milcroft."

"Oh no, you're mistaken. Our dear mutual friend, Ricky, has gone back to Quoon."

"Back to Quoon?" echoed Gay; her heart jerked. "Good God — but why?"

"To find you, my dear. But he's missed the boat, hasn't he? He should have waited. Added to which he is ill, and if he and his friends get to Quoon alive, Li Matin will see that they don't get *out* of it alive. In other words he has gone to certain death."

Gay stared at her speechlessly. Kurt Mulheim's hand closed over hers.

"Don't listen to this rubbish. Come along, Gay. Mr. Morrell can be of no more interest to you. You are coming with me to Johannesburg."

Gay's beautiful eyes turned to him blindly. He was trying to pull her into the hotel. Of course, he expected her to keep her word and to marry him. But Rick had gone back to Quoon to save her. Back to Quoon to face torture and death, for *her* sake. She must do something about it.

15

IT struck Gay in that moment that she loved Rick Morrell more than she had ever loved anybody in her life. Those few hours of understanding, sweet sympathy, between them in Quoon had bred in her a genuine love for him. She loved him, and when a woman loves a man the great outstanding factor of her devotion is self-sacrifice.

As soon as she heard from Lydia that Rick had gone back to face danger, perhaps death, in order to rescue her, she, in her turn, wanted to save him at any cost.

At all costs his life must be saved. She would not want to live if she learned Rick Morrell had died a horrible death in Quoon in the gallant effort to rescue her.

She thought over what Lydia had just told her and asked herself, dizzily, why Rick had done this. Could he have cared a little for her? Yes, that must be so.

Combined with chivalry — the natural feeling of an Englishman that he could not leave a countrywoman to her fate amongst Chinese.

With eyes full of despair, Gay looked at Lydia. Surely, if Lydia cared for Rick, if she had ever loved him in the past, she, too, could not stand by and see Rick go to certain death?

Useless for her to appeal to Kurt Mulheim. His only thought and object was to force her into this marriage which she dreaded and feared. He would not want to save the man she loved.

Gay made a desperate bid for Rick's safety and, lowering pride, forgetting past differences, she appealed to the other woman.

"Mrs. Milcroft — for God's sake — help me save Rick. He's gone back for me, you say. That will be to torture, to something worse than death, if he gets into Li Matin's hands. Mrs. Milcroft — *for God's sake*, help me save him!"

"Help you save him — for you!" Lydia gave a harsh laugh and shook her head. "You ask too much. I happen to want him myself."

196

"Then save him for yourself," said Gay, feverishly. And she added, in reckless passion, "Listen — if you will help me get back to Quoon to rescue him — I'll give myself up to Li Matin. He wanted to marry me. He will still want me, perhaps . . . and let me live. But if he gets Rick into his hands, he'll murder him. Mrs. Milcroft . . . " She clung to the other girl's arm. "You're rich, clever, powerful out here. You can get to Quoon. For heaven's sake, I implore you, help me to rescue Rick, and I swear by every oath I hold sacred that I'll surrender to Li Matin once we reach Quoon."

Mulheim, who was listening in astonishment and fury, began in a blustering voice.

"Look here . . . "

"Be quiet," broke in Lydia. She was flushed and her eyes glittered excitedly. Gay's heroic offer did not stir her to pity, but it bred an idea in her — a fresh scheme. She knew quite well that if Rick chanced to return from Quoon alive, he would never rest until he had found Gay. He might even imagine himself in love with the girl and ask her to marry him.

197

Lydia knew that Rick's feeling for Gay was deeper than he had at first confessed. When he had rushed to Quoon thinking he was going to her rescue, he had been filled with remorse for leaving her there, crazy to get to her and tell her he knew the truth from Ho Kuang, and realized that she was the innocent victim of the plot with Kurt Mulheim.

Even if Gay went to Johannesburg and married Kurt, Rick might follow her and try to take her away. She, Lydia thought, would then lose her last chance of getting him.

"Look here, Mrs. Milcroft — " began Mulheim, livid, snarling.

He got no further. Lydia suddenly spoke to him in German, and what she said caused an expression of almost comical dismay to come across Mulheim's plump features. He sank into complete silence and stared at her with round wide-open eyes. Then Lydia turned to Gay.

"There is something in what you say. I think that you alone might save this young fool who has gone back to Quoon to rescue you. These two men whom he has taken with him . . . they will, of course, be murdered. And he will be murdered too, unless we get there first."

"Then we *must* manage it," said Gay. "We must go to the police. We must rouse the whole town. Ligati and Quoon ought to be wiped out. For God's sake let's go to the Consul at once."

Lydia gripped her arm.

"You're only asking for trouble. If Li Matin lives and hears that the entire British Army were approaching to wipe out Quoon, he would slit Rick Morrell's throat. No, we dare not go for help to the police nor let them interfere. We'll have to do this thing alone, and in our own way."

Gay's heart leapt. At the same time, a tinge of admiration crept into her eyes as she looked at this woman, so lovely, so cool, so resourceful. She wondered if there were anything that Lydia Milcroft could not do.

"Go to your hotel," said Lydia. "Rest there. You'll want some sleep, then pack, and have food, and I will pick you up when it is dark."

"Why can't we go now? Why must we

delay?" began Gay in agony.

"Do as I tell you," said Lydia. "I know what I'm about. Rick and his friends have gone over the desert in the usual way. But there's a *water-way* . . . and I tell you we'll be in Quoon before him."

"And what about Mr. Mulheim? . . ." Gay looked nervously at the German.

Lydia smiled.

"Mr. Mulheim will do as I say."

Gay did not wait to question her further, nor had she any interest in figuring out how it was possible for Lydia to control Mulheim. She went back to her hotel.

She felt that it was essential she should try to get some rest. Certainly she needed it. Her brain was in a turmoil. She was frantic with fear for Rick, and at the same time found it was so marvellous, so touching, to know that he had gone back to Quoon *for her.* He could not be so interested in Lydia after all. He could not altogether believe ill of her, Gay. Anyhow, whatever he believed, he had wanted to save her — if he could.

Lydia Milcroft stood in the sunshine, her parasol shading her red head, and conversed rapidly with Kurt Mulheim for several minutes.

He was no longer dictatorial or blustering. He took on a servile and whining attitude.

"Had I known that it was *you*, Baroness . . . "

"Nobody," interrupted Lydia Milcroft, "knows that I am X.41, nor that my work in London in recent years, in America and out here, is of even greater importance, my dear Herr Mulheim, than your own. I regret to have to remove your lady friend. It is a loss which you must suffer for the moment. Although, perhaps, we can form a plan together which will enable you to get her back, once her job in Quoon is done."

He spread out his podgy fingers.

"I care deeply for her, and I thought she would be useful to me in my . . . in our work for our Fuehrer."

Lydia laughed.

"Oh, she is pretty and stupid enough to be very useful. But perhaps you over-estimate her value. The value of Mr. Morrell is, however, extraordinary. Apart from my personal feeling for him,

Herr Mulheim, he is an engineer of considerable brilliance. It was unfortunate and necessary for me to break with him in London some time back and go out to Chicago. I needed the money. My orders from headquarters were to accept Roger Milcroft. At the same time, I do not forget that when I met Morrell, his work was in a certain aircraft factory in England, and he once had access to plans which would be of vital interest to us in Germany. No doubt he can no longer get those plans, but he can still remember them and use his brain — for me."

Mulheim gnawed at his finger-nails.

"Do you think Morrell would betray his country?"

"Not willingly. But a little dope . . . a little gentle persuasion, the arts of which you know so well, Herr Mulheim . . . and we shall see."

Mulheim regarded her with respect, but was not yet happy about having Gay torn from him like this at the very hour when victory had seemed in sight. At the same time, he was powerless. X.41 was not to be argued with, but to be listened to and respected. She had a position about that of Herr Mulheim himself. He must be subordinate to her and her wishes.

Lydia smiled at him sweetly.

"Do not despair, my friend. When we have done our work for the Fatherland, we may yet have time for our hearts' personal desires. Let us discuss ways and means."

Standing there on the verandah, they stayed talking in their own language.

They might have been two innocent tourists. Nobody knew who they were. Nobody cared.

An hour later, with all the luggage they needed — light packs for the coolie servants to carry — and both girls dressed in riding kit and wearing solar topees, Gay Burnett and Lydia left the busy coastal town for Quoon.

This time, they did not go across the desert. Lydia, with all the resources at her command, had made close enquiries and discovered that they could travel by boat up the river as far as Ligati, and that it would in fact be a better, less strenuous route. Thence, in another boat — possibly a Chinese junk — they could get to Quoon.

Lydia, having made up her mind to get Rick Morrell for herself and the services of the country that was, in fact, her Fatherland, saw it through to the bitter end. She was rich — her late husband had left her a fortune — and great riches can achieve much in this world. Couples with good looks, a smart brain, it could do practically everything here, and it might mean ultimate glory for her with her Fuehrer, if she could eventually pick Morrell's brains.

A Eurasian, captain of the small cargo boat going up to Ligati with cotton-bales, accepted a handsome bribe from Lydia and allowed the two girls on board. With them went six of Lydia's coolies — trusted men who had been under German influence and serving German masters in Liberia for years. They were virtually Lydia's slaves, ready to go to hell for her. She knew neither their language nor their ways, but the foreman could interpret for her. She acted with a cool precision which Gay was forced to admire.

"Do you think there is a real chance

of our saving Rick?" Gay asked Lydia, feverishly. And Lydia answered:

"Yes — don't worry — we shall save him."

Once on the cargo boat, a period of terror and discomfort commenced for Gay. She was given a small cabin — a stifling compartment with a sailors' hard bunk. In here she had to eat, sleep, and spend all the long hot days and the scarcely less scorching nights.

The turgid river looked like oil, its glassy surface reflecting the brilliance of the starlit skies. Now and then the vegetation on the river banks was so thick that lianas met and twined overhead, making a green archway over the slowly moving boat.

Lydia deliberately kept Gay in her cabin.

"It isn't safe for you to come out. I know these people and their ways. I can manage them. They are afraid of me. But you must stay here. I will lock you in and keep the key. You will come to some harm, otherwise."

Gay made no protest. She was past resistance and too desperately worried to care what became of her. She bore the terrible heat, the lack of air and exercise, and poor food, stoically. She was doing this for Rick whom she loved, and who was trying to save her. A dozen times she pictured him, his tall lithe figure, his brown gaunt face and those attractive eyes. Eyes which had smiled at her. Arms which had held her once, in Li Matin's palace. Sensitive fingers which had smoothed her hair. She loved him with a great passion. A passionate renunciation. She could not endure that he should be put to the torture and murdered in Quoon. She must get to him — save him — at any price. He would be happy again with Lydia, whom he loved. Friend, angel, whichever she was.

Beyond his rescue, she dared look no further, dared not dwell on the idea of her own personal danger and her surrender to that horrible Chinaman. Her fate would not be as kind as death. She refused to think about it. She brooded over the memory of Rick and the hope of saving him.

She did not wish him to know of her sacrifice. She dared not let him know.

Otherwise, as Lydia had pointed out, he would not accept her sacrifice. He would prefer death at Li Matin's hands.

Night after night, when the sky blazed with stars and the cargo boat crept down the dark, oily waters through the wild plains of Africa towards Ligati, Gay lay tossing feverishly on her bunk. And sometimes when she was only half-conscious or only when she slept, did a grain of comfort come. Her dream of Rick holding her to his heart. And then, indeed, sacrifice seemed worth while, and courage returned to her.

16

THERE came another of those dreadful, terrifying nights when Gay was alone in her cabin, and Lydia was out on deck controlling her queer subordinates. The cargo boat stopped at Zamboli, an unimportant river town, for fuel and fresh provisions.

On to the boat came a tall European wearing dungarees, white shirt, and with a pack over his back, a revolver and cartridges in a leather belt about his waist. He wore the usual sun-helmet on his head. A thin, haggard Englishman with a weary face and bloodshot eyes. He looked ill and worn, as though he had not slept for nights, and wanted a wash and shave badly. He went straight to the tiny cabin given to him by the Captain. The Eurasian was doing well out of fares given him by these Europeans this particular trip, and he was pleased. The Englishman flung himself on his bunk and slept without moving for many hours. He did not appear on deck until the boat was steaming up-river again.

Lydia, standing by the rails, smoking a cigarette, was cursing the heat and the mosquitoes. She would be glad when this damnable journey was over. But if Gay could be put safely out of the way in Quoon, and Rick recover his faith in her, it was all well worth while, she thought.

She saw the tall Englishman strolling along deck under the canvas awning which protected them from the fierce sunlight during the day. She gave a violent start. *Rick*. Good heavens, Rick, himself!

She saw in a flash what had happened. He had gone across desert as far as Zamboli, left his police escort there, and had joined the cargo boat alone. He had obviously made plans and decided that it would be best for him to return one way and the two men to take the cross-country route, to ensure the safe arrival of at least one of them.

Lydia flung away her cigarette.

"Ricky!" she cried.

He saw and recognized Lydia, and stopped dead. His whole body stiffened.

She saw, at once, bitter hostility in his eyes. Of course — after all that fool Ho Kuang had told him — she was out of favour with Rick.

"What the hell are *you* doing on this boat?" he demanded tersely. He was far from pleased to see her and did not intend to pretend that he was in any way glad.

He knew now the harm which she had done both Gay and himself. She was the most wicked woman he had ever imagined possible. And if the police reports were correct, she was also one of the most unscrupulous and dangerous spies under the Nazi regime. She stood there, looking as lovely as ever. So cool, so attractive, physically. But Rick Morrell loathed and despised her as much as he had once adored.

Her long lashes drooped. Her cunning brain, as usual, worked on rapid lines. She saw that she must do two things. One, ingratiate herself back into Rick's favour. The other, prevent him from knowing that Gay was on board. At all costs, she must do *that*. It would ruin things for her if they were to meet, and he were to know how courageously the young girl had offered herself as a hostage for him.

She must lie, Lydia decided. Lie for all she was worth. She would tell Rick that Gay had died. Died on her way back from Quoon. She could easily manage to keep Gay a prisoner in her cabin, and with the aid of dope and her many native servants, as soon as they touched Ligati, she would have Gay spirited away, never to be seen alive again by Rick Morrell.

Utterly without mercy, an unscrupulous criminal working on behalf of the German government, Lydia Milcroft formed her plan to get this man.

She assumed an appealing attitude.

"Rick," she said, "I know you are thinking awful things of me — but you misjudge me. I — "

"There is no question of misjudging," broke in Rick, "What you have done is unpardonable. You have tried to kill Gay Burnett. I don't mind what you've done to me. But what you did to her was a crime. Do you realize just what you *did* do? Leaving that young white girl in that unspeakable place — in the hands of a fellow like Kurt Mulheim? I was fool enough to believe what you said when you told me you were not in the scheme. But, my God, now I know the truth. Your ally, Ho Kuang, enlightened me."

Lydia bit her lips. She smiled, a slow strange smile. In that bell-like voice, so like a child's, she said:

"Rick, I can see you are thinking the very worst of me, but I'm not responsible for anything that happened to Gay Burnett. I'm terribly sorry if Ho Kuang led you astray about her. He's a liar and after cash. He thought he'd get more out of you if he lied about me, and — "

"I don't want to discuss it — or to have anything to do with you," broke in Rick harshly. "I don't believe one single word you say."

He was a tired and still a sick man. And he was a prey, night and day, to the most agonizing remorse — for having left Gay in Quoon. He knew now that she meant more to him than Lydia had ever meant. He was ready to go through hell in order to find her and bring her back to safety. He had been blind and mad to allow Lydia to deceive him. He had only one thought and aim now — to get to Quoon, find Gay, and tell her how much he loved her. Yes, he was in love with her, and wanted to spend the rest of his life in proving it. He would never touch a drop of drink in his life. All that was finished. Lydia hadn't been worth the flinging away of his life. He would regain his self-respect and his position in England — with Gay.

Lydia burst into tears.

"Rick, Rick, please don't turn from me like this. I love you."

"For God's sake, don't drag up that ancient lie."

"Rick — you can't be so cruel. Don't you realize that I am on this boat for the very same purpose as you yourself?"

"What do you mean?"

"I am on this boat because I regret any harm that has come to Gay Burnett. I mean that I am going to Quoon to try to save her . . . "

Rick looked at Lydia doubtfully. Was that a fact? Could he trust her — after all her treachery? And she thought:

"Tonight I must give Gay plenty of

213

dope . . . and see that she stays quiet till we get to Ligati. She mustn't be seen or heard . . . "

"Yes, I'm going to try and save Gay. So for heaven's sake, let us be friends and work together," she said. "Otherwise we'll both fail. We must work together, Ricky."

He hesitated. His gaze wandered restlessly out at the dark, glassy water . . . at the distant desert, and on one side the sinister fringe of jungle. Then he looked round the deck again, trying to make up his mind whether or not to believe in this woman who had betrayed him so and treated Gay with such utter lack of scruple, of womanly sympathy.

Suddenly the blood rushed to his cheeks. He caught his breath and almost cried out. But, by a superhuman effort, he checked himself. Every nerve in his body was tingling. Over Lydia's golden head he saw a porthole . . . and through that porthole a pale, agonized young face stared hopelessly out at the moonlight.

It was Gay. Gay was there — in that cabin — actually on this boat. Gay, whom he had been told was still in Quoon. And this woman, this unspeakable creature, whom he had once loved, was trying to bluff him, to pretend that she was his friend and that she, too, was bent on the rescue of Gay.

In that moment, Rick Morrell made up his mind that in order to defeat Lydia, he must meet cunning with cunning. She wanted to keep him from Gay. She was bent on Gay's destruction. Very well. *He must not let her know that he knew that Gay was on board.* And he would wait and watch and act when the chance offered itself.

The pale young face — a face he had dreamed about and longed for during his illness — vanished. Shivering with excitement Rick lit a cigarette.

"Very well, Lydia, we will be friends," he said deliberately.

She was unaware that he had caught a glimpse of Gay. She smiled triumphantly, put an arm through his, and walked with him down the deck. She was confident that she was going to win him in the end. It would be easier than she had imagined.

But Rick — his brain working furiously — was thinking:

"She's too damned subtle. It will need subtlety to outwit her. Gay and I have got to get away — *together.* But the question is — how is it going to be done?

Gay had not seen Rick Morrell board the boat. The dark, solitary hours, the long days, passed . . . dragged wretchedly for her. She remained in the cabin. Nobody came to her. Lydia visited her at intervals. Always cool, confident, still advising Gay to remain safely where she was. It was not part of Lydia's plan to allow Gay to see Rick on this boat. So, through the interminable hours, Gay waited alone. Up and down the tiny cabin which imprisoned her, up and down, hopelessly, hopelessly.

Another day passed . . . and another night. Gay felt that she passed from one dark and sinister dream to another. Nobody came to her now except servants who gave her food and drink and vanished again. For twenty-four hours now, Lydia had not come. Gay made up her mind that unless Lydia came back she would attract the Captain's attention from the porthole. She could not, would not endure this cruel isolation. She was terrified and alone, and she did not know, could not guess what Lydia had up her sleeve.

That night the cargo boat docked at Ligati. Gay, exhausted after sleepless hours the night before, did not know that they had reached Ligati. She did not even hear the clatter of cargo being taken off by native sailors when they were in port.

At two in the morning, everybody on board was sleeping. Ligati and the market square, scene of the great market, lay quiet under the moon. But one person was wide awake. Rick . . . Rick, who for twenty-four hours had been humouring Lydia, waiting his chance to rescue Gay and get off this boat. Longing for a word with the girl, a chance to restore her confidence.

Lydia was in her own cabin, sleeping. At dawn she had planned to take Rick Morrell to Quoon and there he would be told that Gay had died. Some proof, some article of her clothing could be given to prove it. But in the darkness, those silent watches just before dawn, Rick crept noiselessly through the boat and found Gay's cabin. He unlocked the door and turned the handle.

"Gay! Gay!" he whispered.

Instantly she was awake. She sat up on the bunk, startled, staring before her. A shaft of moonlight through the porthole showed him her white thin little face. She looked unspeakably forlorn and pathetic to him. She put a coat around her thin young shoulders and sprang quickly from the bed. The next instant she had reached his side, and he opened his arms to receive her.

"Gay, my poor little sweet!" he said.

She did not stop to wonder how this miracle had occurred. She only knew that Rick's arms were about her once again. He was wiping out the terror, the loneliness, the despair. And she knew that he, too, was safe. Frantically she clung to him.

"Rick — oh, Rick — Rick!" she said.

Their lips met and clung in a long kiss. But even as Gay touched the fringe of that heaven, it was snatched from her. A shadow moved behind Rick, a thin brown arm reached out from the darkness, brought something down upon

218

his head. It was a sickening blow. Gay saw, heard, and screamed. Wild with terror. She felt Rick Morrell's tall body sag and drop in the circle of her arms. Then soundlessly he dropped on to the cabin floor.

17

SO quietly and soundlessly he dropped at her feet, she scarcely had time to think. Her straining arms — too slight, too weak for such a weight — could not hold him. He lay like a dead thing against her feet. The brown shadow that had defeated Rick's purpose had vanished as stealthily and unexpectedly as it had come. For a few moments Gay thought that Rick was dead. That cruel and cowardly blow had surely killed him. She shut her eyes and then stared dumbly at his body. She was physically sick with the horror and the disappointment. Then a light flashed on in her cabin. She lifted her dazed eyes again and saw, as through a mist, the face of her old enemy, Kurt Mulheim. She had not dreamed that he was on this boat. He stood there in her doorway. It seemed to the girl in that moment that there was no end to this nightmare. Just as she had found Rick again and his arms had closed about her, his lips reviving all her hopes, her strength, the old horror descended on her once again.

Mulheim was on board, once more ready to pursue and persecute. It was almost more than she could bear. She gave a heartbreaking cry. But the next moment Mulheim was at her side. He caught her arm and steadied her swaying young figure.

Her frantic cry of *"Rick! Rick!"* was stifled when Mulheim laid a plump hand across her lips.

"No, *Liebchen* . . . no use to call a dead man . . . better to embrace a living one," said his low, guttural voice in her ear. Then he added something incomprehensible to her. Two native servants sprang into the cabin and with their thin strong fingers bound her ankles and wrists. Mulheim, himself, put a gag in her mouth. She was helpless and only half conscious when they carried her out of that cabin, stepping over the prostrate form of Rick Morrell.

On to the deck they took her, the two men carrying her, the German whispering his orders.

Moonlight . . . the uncanny stillness of the African night . . . the faint musky scent of the river that ran like smooth oil, glittering under the cold clear stars.

Everybody in that cargo boat slept, with the exception of the Captain, who watched what was going on, unmoved. His pockets were stuffed with crisp notes. Mulheim had paid him well to anchor the boat at Ligati for another quarter of an hour. There was a white motorboat rocking alongside, which received Mulheim and his servants, and Gay's half-conscious form.

Only a few whispering voices . . . the lapping of water against the boat . . . and the sudden chug-chug of the motor-boat cutting a way through the turgid river towards the dark shore.

The cargo boat moved on towards Quoon. Rick Morrell lay where he had fallen, in the doorway of Gay's cabin. His white face was hidden on the curve of his arm, and the blood trickled slowly from a wound on the side of his head.

Gay, capable of neither moving nor speaking, knew absolute and complete despair. When full consciousness returned she could see . . . and she knew what was going on about her. She could not guess at the fate in store for her. Mulheim had in some way defeated Lydia. She supposed he must be still crazy to force her into his arms. She believed that nothing and nobody could prevent him from taking her now, where he wished, and that he would give her no further opportunity to escape.

She was carried from the river bank into Ligati, through the dark, sleeping village, through the bazaar. She passed that terrible market square which she saw and recognized with a thrill of horror, and into a small wooden house with a verandah running round it. Lights gleamed in the windows. It was a native 'rest-house' run by an old woman, a Eurasian with Dutch and Negro blood in her. She spoke a kind of bastard German and was eager and willing to do what Mulheim wished. He had good money to offer. She was ready to house the English girl and to see that she did not get away.

A more repulsive woman Gay had never seen. Brown-skinned, thick-lipped, blind in one eye, she had also all the worst traits of the two races in her character. She took Gay to an apology for a bedroom, a dirty room, hot and squalid. Everything was rotten, had rotted with the damp heat. Gay felt sure that the walls were crawling with insects. The one small window was heavily barred. From here, there could be no escape. Yet another stage of torture was about to begin, Gay told herself, and felt cold with fear.

Her ankles and wrists were untied. The gag was removed from her mouth. Once the old woman had shut the door and left her with Mulheim, Gay, with all the strength she had left, asked for an explanation of this new catastrophe which had overtaken her.

"You won't leave me here. You can't. For God's sake, if you have a spark of decency in you, let me go." she said.

The German smiled. He liked to see Gay on her knees. It satisfied him. She was going to be kept on her knees, too, metaphorically speaking, he thought. He was sick of asking Gay for favours. He had changed his tactics. He would never forgive or forget the fact that Lydia Milcroft had taken her away from him. But he had thwarted Lydia. X.41 no longer commanded respect, nor did he need to accept her orders. A cable to Berlin had brought him a satisfactory reply. X.41 was out of favour with the Gestapo. She had had several failures lately. They were not interested in Rick Morrell. She was overcome by her passion for him, rather than working on behalf of her country. Kurt Mulheim was satisfied that he could go ahead with his own plans and disregard the woman. That was the worst of women spies. So often their personal feelings overcame their sense of loyalty, of patriotism.

"Don't waste breath, Fräulein, because I don't intend to let you go this time," he told Gay abruptly. "You shall stay here until your spirit is broken, and until you *beg* me to take you into my arms and *beg* me to take you to Johannesburg and make you my wife!"

Gay rose to her feet. She trembled violently. But she flung back her head with a gesture of defiance.

"Very well. I'd rather stay here than

225

beg you to marry me," she said. "And I am never going to marry you now that I know Rick is safe."

Mulheim lit his pipe. He shrugged his shoulders. In the faint down light which filtered through the barred window, his face was merciless. She looked at him and her heart quailed. What mercy could she expect from such a fiend as this man? He said:

"Then you are very foolish, *Liebchen*, because, for every insult you give me, for every refusal, for every look of scorn, you shall pay. You shall stay here with old Greta — who is my loyal servant — and there will be guards on all sides of this bungalow, and no possible chance of escape for you. You shall be starved and neglected. Your spirit shall be broken . . . *broken*, I say . . . " His voice sank to a savage whisper. He gripped her wrists. "I thought you a child, an easily managed child. But there is tigress in you also. I like the tigress. She fascinates me. But I do not wish to take her too forcibly. She shall come willingly to my embrace and she shall be grateful that she has Kurt Mulheim as her master."

Gay shrank away, her heart pounding madly with fear.

"Oh, God, I think you're mad. You and Lydia Milcroft are both mad."

"I am only mad with the desire to break you and put an end to this whining and shrinking," he said fiercely. "You escaped from one marriage — but the next you shall come to willingly, as you shall see."

"Oh, Rick," she said under her breath, "Rick."

"Little fool — you call a dead man."

"He isn't dead — he isn't."

"If he isn't — he soon will be. If he reached Quoon alive with that woman, Lydia Milcroft — that failure of a spy — neither of them will live long . . . " Mulheim laughed. "Li Matin and his men will be waiting for them. And your good-looking Englishman, Rick, will be put to death for the attempted murder of the Mandarin. He won't be so good-looking when they've finished with him . . . those Chinese devils . . . "

Gay reeled. Mulheim caught her close. He went on ruthlessly describing to her the ghastly death Rick would die. It completely unnerved her. He picked her up in his arms and laid her on the camp-bed, sweeping aside the dirty netting. He said:

"Poor little *Liebchen* — so difficult to tame! But it will be all the sweeter for the waiting. Our life together will be excellent. A woman should always be subservient. You are going to offer me your sweetness of your own free will. Till then you stay here. But do not be stubborn too long, *Liebchen*. It will only hurt you. In the end you will be conquered. You will call for poor Kurt who loves you."

He looked down at the prostrate young figure on the camp-bedstead. Outside, dawn was breaking. Fair, lovely rose, blue, and gold over the savage and sinister country. It was cooler now than at any time of day. Gay lay on the bed with closed eyes, her courage fast ebbing from her. She felt Mulheim's lips against her hand. She shuddered. She knew that she would not be able to stand much more pain and terror and that she would either give way to this madman, or die. She wondered if they were going to torture her, starve her here. She had heard that the Nazis thought nothing of torture. If so, how could she hold out? She was weak physically. She loved Rick Morrell. That long kiss they had exchanged on the boat had bound her forever to him. But if this German maniac broke her courage, she might have to crawl to him in the end. The thought filled her with shame and loathing.

Mulheim left her. She raised herself from the bed, and with what strength was left in her staggered to the window. Through the bars the air smelled sweeter than in this noisome room. She could see, in the dawn-light, a wild, desolate, neglected garden burnt by the hot sunshine. Beyond the dark lay the shadow of Ligati. The native kraals and the bazaar. It looked unearthly in the pearly dawn. The girl was seized with an indescribable sense of loneliness. She felt deserted by God and man. She tried to concentrate on the memory of Rick and his strong arms holding her, his voice saying. "Gay, poor little sweet." His hands caressing her hair. He loved her a little after all. He cared whether she lived or died. He had meant to take her off that boat, and in the attempt had been struck down. Was he dead? It couldn't be true. Surely he was alive. Was he dead, or going on to a cruel death in Quoon, hoping to find her there? If he no longer lived, she would pray to die. She sank down on the floor by the window and leaned her head against her arm. The burning tears dripped slowly from her eyes down her pale little face. She whispered:

"Rick, Rick . . . are you dead or living? Oh, my dear, my dear, I'd have died for you so willingly."

She was very thirsty. Her throat ached and burned. There was no water in this room. The door was locked. There was no sound from outside. Mulheim had gone. The old woman, Greta, was perhaps asleep. It was the dawn, the most silent and desolate hour in Ligati. But the moment the sun blazed out, the village would awake. The savage, cruel day would begin again.

For Gay there was no sleep possible. She crouched by her window, haggard, trying to pray. Now and then she started violently, disturbed by the sudden rustle of a small lizard scuttling across the floor into a hole, or a centipede dropping from the ceiling. She was repelled by the thought of snakes, of creeping insects. She wondered how long she would prefer them to Kurt Mulheim.

Suddenly she was roused by a rustling sound outside her window. She sprang up and looked out, wide-eyed, frightened. What was there? What fresh terror lay in store for her?

And then every drop of blood seemed to pump madly through her body. Her heart jumped. She saw a face at her window — a brown familiar face. Rick Morrell. Rick with a white scarf wound around his head, serving as a bandage. But Rick, nevertheless, *alive*.

Wild with joy, Gay clung to the window bars.

"Rick, Rick! Oh, my very dear!"

"Ssh," he whispered, "quiet, for God's sake! Yes, yes, I'm all right, sweet, don't cry."

"Oh, Rick . . . Rick!" The tears were pelting down her cheeks. He looked at her hungrily and tried to reach that poor, wet little face through the bars, with one hand. "My poor sweet — do you love me, my dear?"

"Yes, yes," she said brokenly. "I'm terribly in love with you, Rick. Oh, darling. I thought you were dead . . . "

"No. That blow only stunned me. Then when I recovered, I dived overboard and swam ashore. I made enquiries and a black who'd seen you come off the motor-boat told me where to find you. He had watched the three men carry you here. Who are they? Who does this foul place belong to?"

"A Eurasian woman in Mulheim's pay. It was Mulheim who took me off the ship. He means to break me this time. You've got to get me away."

"He won't break you," said Rick grimly. "But listen, darling. This bungalow is being watched. I can't get in to let you out. I've been hiding, watching for a chance to slip away before they're on the alert. I'll come back tonight when it's dark. Here is a file. Hide it carefully. If you can file these bars away, fix them so they look O.K. if anyone comes. Then get through when I give you the signal.

I'll be ready for you. Whistle for me three times when you're alone and you think it safe. My pals who left with me have been murdered. But I know the doctor here. He's half-caste but reliable. The police told me his name. I'm going to bribe him to help us get away."

Nothing could have given Gay more courage and more happiness than those words. It was so grand to know he was alive, to feel the warmth and comfort of his hand through the bars, holding hers. She bent and kissed thoses hands of his in an excess of joy and love. He said huskily:

"Oh, my sweet little Gay. When this nightmare ends, I'm going to be very different for your sake. We're going to love each other a hell of a lot, and go back to England together."

"There'll never be anybody else on earth for me but you, Rick. I'm crazy about you."

"I've discovered that I love you a whole lot," he said. "But I must go — I daren't stay. It's too light now. But I'll be waiting and watching."

"Bless you, Rick. And, if luck is with

233

us tonight, we'll soon be together again."

"Yes, we can only hope," he said.

He kissed her thin small fingers passionately. Then she let him go. He disappeared from sight and she was alone. But with new courage, new hope, and the feeling that she would do and dare anything on earth for this man who dared so much for her sake.

Never, now, would she give way to that German fiend. She belonged to Rick. It was going to be Rick now or death.

18

MORNING had come. The sun was high, and the African earth baked and cracked under the fierce glare of it. In Ligati the merchants gathered round the slave market and the bazaar hummed and buzzed with traders. In Gay's sordid prison a very different girl from the hopeless and despairing one of last night, faced that new day. She had slept for a few hours. She felt fresh and strong again. Old Greta had brought her food and drink. Very little, and what there was, of obnoxious quality. But it was sufficient to keep Gay alive. She forced herself to eat because life meant Rick Morrell to her now. Mulheim came to see her, and was astonished at the curious change in his captive. She greeted him calmly. There was a brightness in her soft blue eyes, a colour in her hollowed cheeks, something which suggested to him that she had changed her policy with regard to him. She was going to be sensible, perhaps, and give in — without further trouble.

Perhaps a few hours in this unattractive bedroom had influenced her.

"You realize that life will be more pleasant if you come willingly to do exactly as I tell you, don't you, *meine Liebe?*" he murmured, eyeing her with interest. "Come — you need not stay here another hour. If you will just beg me to take you, to teach you what life can mean in my arms."

She returned his gaze bravely, and some of the colour left her face. Somehow she managed to smile. She shrugged her shoulders with a suggestion of despair.

"I don't quite know what to do."

He came to her and took her in his arms.

"Let me tell you what to do," he whispered, and kissed her on the lips.

For an instant she endured that embrace. But her right hand stole into his pocket and closed over the butt of a revolver, a little pocket revolver which Mulheim always carried. Then quickly and with a new courage born of her love for Rick Morrell, she sprang back from him and pointed the revolver at her head.

"If you touch me again, I'll shoot myself. I swear it — and you can believe that I mean what I say!" she cried.

Mulheim swore under his breath. Baffled and disappointed, he stared at her. The little devil, he thought, getting his revolver like that, confound her. Just when he had thought she was on the verge of surrender. He took a step forward, but her eyes flashed so warningly that he stopped.

"I swear it — I'll put a bullet through my head and then you will take my dead body," she said.

He hesitated. Yes, he could see that she meant what she said. He did not want her dead body. He wanted the living, breathing Gay in his arms.

"Very well," he said. "You win — for the moment, Fräulein. But we shall see who will be the one to conquer in the end."

He turned and walked out of the room, bolting it behind him. Gay relaxed and shut her eyes. Her whole body dripped with perspiration. But she did not let go of the revolver. Precious weapon! It meant so much. It would serve as her own protection; and now that Mulheim had left her, she could use the file Rick had given her and sever these bars.

She wasted no time. Panting, flushed with triumph, she set to work on the bars of her prison window. To make room for her to get through tonight was all that she needed. Enough room to let her get through when Rick came back for her tonight. She had filed through three bars. These would be sufficient space, when they were moved, to enable her to get through on to the verandah. Mad with hope, she replaced the bars, in case Mulheim or old Greta came in, and saw what she had done. She must wait for darkness, to aid the escape.

That day seemed interminable. The sun set, a great scarlet disc on the western horizon. The temperature grew more tolerable. Then fell the swift and sudden darkness, and Gay walked up and down her little room, up and down, listening, waiting, hoping.

When would Rick come?

She whistled three times, softly . . . as

he had told her. She did so with the blood turning to ice in her veins. Terror-stricken in case Mulheim heard, or one of the negro guards came on the scene, and Rick would be found and finished off finally.

The hours went by. Rick did not come.

The feverish hope, the excitement of the day, gradually faded, and Gay's very soul grew deadly tired of waiting. Something must have happened Rick. If he were alive and free, she knew that he would come.

Then somebody unbolted her door. She stood panting, big-eyed, desperate. Old Greta came in.

"You wanted next door," she croaked, leering at the girl. "Come 'long . . . "

Gay went, and despair settled on her soul once more. But she gripped her revolver with cold and shaking hand. She had really not the slightest idea how to use it. Never before in her life had she handled firearms. But if there were going to be any trouble with Mulheim, she would do her best.

Old Greta pushed her unceremoniously

into a room on the other side of the bungalow. It was cleaner than the wretched bedroom in which Gay had been imprisoned. The walls were whitewashed and harsh, unshaded lights were shining. Standing by a table on which there were food and drink, was Kurt Mulheim.

But Gay did not see him. She saw only the tall figure of the man beside him. And then she knew that their plan had failed. Rick was there. His hands were tied behind him. He was smiling at her as though with encouragement. But in his eyes there was bitter disappointment.

Gay raised her revolver and said in an hysterical voice:

"Let him go. Let us both go, Mr. Mulheim, or I'll shoot you dead. I swear I will."

But she was not quick enough. She had been too dazed. A shadow stole behind her and a hand knocked the automatic from hers.

With a chuckling laugh Mulheim advanced and picked up his revolver.

"I must teach you something about shooting, *Leibchen*," he said, "just as I must teach tactics to your — shall we call him — friend, Mr. Morrell. He had made plans to rescue you — most gallantly. Unfortunately for him, I outwitted those plans, and now you shall decide what is to be done with him."

Rick set his teeth. His eyes spoke volumes to Gay. "Sorry, sweet," he said. "I've let you down badly."

She stumbled to him and put her arms around his neck. A broken sob came from her.

"Oh, my darling."

"Sorry, sweet," repeated, his face grey in the garish light which was reflected from the whitewashed walls. "I just couldn't make it. But I love you. Every hour that passes I think I love you more."

She ignored the presence of Kurt Mulheim, who was regarding this scene with deep dissatisfaction. Rick could not put his arms about her, but she held him close and lifted her lips to his kiss. Once again she knew in her soul that she loved this man as much as it was possible for a woman to love.

She said:

"If it's to be death, I hope I die with you."

"It will not be death for you, *kleine* Gay," came from Mulheim sharply; "you know what I expect from *you*."

He advanced towards her. She shrank back and put her arms convulsively around Rick. Rick said:

"Oh, God, darling, I can't do a thing. I can't even knock this swine to hell."

Mulheim drew nearer, and with another of his chuckling laughs, caught Gay's arm and dragged her away from the Englishman. Lifting his hand he hit Rick across the mouth. A blow that drew blood.

Frenziedly Gay struggled in Mulheim's hands.

"You coward! You beastly coward to hit a man who can't hit back. Oh, you beast!"

Mulheim kept her in his grip and went on laughing.

"So! The little tigress is roused. I had no idea you were quite as — shall we call it — keen on your English friend. Such a waste of devotion. He is a drink-sodden fool."

Gay looked at Rick. A dark flush had spread over his livid face as he heard the German's last words. His lips were bleeding, but somehow he grinned at Gay.

"Chin up, darling. Don't let that devil get you down."

"He never will, never."

"That," said Mulheim softly, "only time will tell. Meanwhile it may interest you two to know that news has reached me that our two countries are at war."

Gay and Rick exchanged glances. Gay ceased struggling in the German's hands. She said:

"At war?"

"So! The peace of Munich was short-lived. The troops of my Government are even now in Poland. The English Government demanded in their usual insolent fashion that we should withdraw our troops. The Fuehrer refused, so a state of war now exists."

"So much the worse for you and your countrymen," said Rick tersely. "You'll get the licking you deserve."

The German eyed him over the rims of his glasses. "You think so, *hein?* I assure you that you are mistaken. In a short time we shall bring Great Britain to her knees . . . just as I intend to bring this so charming countrywoman of yours to *hers* . . . ”

He bent and kissed Gay full on the lips in front of Rick.

Rick Morrell struggled violently in the hands of the native who was holding him. Gay called to him:

“Don’t bother. I can tackle him. I’ll never give in, Rick. I’ll die first of all.”

Rick glared at the German.

“Yes, and mind you remember, you fat pig, that there’s a song in our country which says ‘Britons never, never, never shall be slaves’.”

“Be quiet,” snarled Mulheim. “And take it from me, my good Morrell, that for me like you, Germany has a very *special* death.”

“God!” said Rick under his breath, trying to get free. “If only I could get at you.”

Mulheim laughed again and drew the shrinking figure of the girl nearer him.

“What a lot of things you would do if you could get away again. What a lot you would give to be in England now, answering the bugle-call, *hein?* Getting into a nice uniform, learning to be a soldier, sticking bayonets into sacks that are supposed to be German soldiers. It caused me immense satisfaction, my dear Morrell, to know that you will never do any of these things, and that the girl you love will remain with me long after the vultures in the desert are picking your bones."

Gay looked bleakly at the Germans.

"What do you mean to do?" she asked.

"Allow you the privilege of watching with me, *Liebchen,* the last moments of your would-be rescuer."

"You can't kill him . . . you can't . . . it will be murder."

"Not at all," said Mulheim. "Remember that our countries are at war and it will be just one German killing one Englishman in self-defence, shall we call it? He would kill *me* if he could."

"That's the first true word you've said, Mulheim," came from Rick.

Gay gave a moan of despair.

"Rick, what in God's name can we do?"

Mulheim answered her harshly.

"You can do nothing. I will teach you to prefer this Englishman's kisses to mine!"

Still keeping her imprisoned in his grasp, he spoke to Rick.

"You will now be locked up, my good Morrell, until sunrise. After that you will be stripped and bound and left by native servants on a rock in the desert. You will have neither hat nor any protection from the sun. In short time you will go mad from the heat. Later you will die in agony and Gay shall sit with me under cover, and watch your death-throes. She shall wish that she had never been born. And you, my good Morrell, will die begging the German whom you call 'a fat pig' for the mercy that he will not show you . . . "

Mulheim's voice died away. Another voice had broken the silence. The cool clear voice of a woman from the doorway. Mulheim swung round and saw Lydia Milcroft standing there. And now it was his turn to be afraid. The triumph faded from his eyes and the red from his cheeks. His jaw dropped.

246

For Lydia Milcroft was pointing a small shining revolver at him and he knew that X.41 could shoot — and shoot straight.

Gay screamed.

"Mrs. Milcroft! You've come to save us?"

Lydia took no notice of her. She cast a fleeting look at Rick.

"I've come to save *you*," she said . . . then added to Mulheim: "Put up your hands, you double-crossing traitor."

Mulheim started to shake. His plump body was like a jelly. His eyes protruded. He said:

"Baroness, we are friends and countrymen . . . we serve the same leader. You cannot work against me."

"I was ready to work with you," she said in her high clear voice, "until you wormed your way on to that boat and took my two captives ashore."

"I've been keeping Mr. Morrell here for you," whined Mulheim.

"You've been threatening to kill him. I heard every word that you said."

Mulheim licked his lips.

"Baroness . . . I was carried away

247

by my force of love for the Fräulein,
Listen . . . "

He broke into a flood of German.
Gay could not understand, but Rick
knew the language, and while he stood
there, staring blankly at the two, yet
another staggering revelation was made
to him. For not only was Lydia Milcroft
an adventuress, a criminal, who would
not hesitate to send a young white girl
like Gay Burnett to a ghastly fate, she
was a spy. That was the explanation
of her mysterious movements and the
power which she seemed to wield. She
was a Nazi agent known as X.41. She
had been working for the German
Government even in the days when
she had lived at Monte Carlo with her
American employer. London society had
accepted her and her wild stories about
her parentage. But in reality she was
Bavarian, and, from what Rick could
gather during the sharp dispute between
her and Mulheim, the two agents had
fallen out.

Mulheim was growing offensive now,
furiously accusing Lydia of betraying the
interests of the Fatherland for her own

personal desires. He was warning her that, if and when she reached Berlin again, her reception might not be as warm as she hoped.

Lydia laughed.

"You bore me, Mulheim," she said, "and I'm acting in the interests of my country. If I carry out the plans I made when I first came to Africa, mainly to secure the services of my former fiancé, Richard Morrell."

From Rick's bleeding lips there burst a terse protest.

"You'll never have me on your side, Lydia. I know too much about you now."

She eyed him through her long lashes, but kept Mulheim covered.

"You and I will learn to understand each other better when we are away from all this pandemonium," she said smoothly.

Gay reached the woman's side.

"Mrs. Milcroft, help us to get away, please."

Lydia looked at her coldly.

"You are an English fool and I have no use for you," she said.

"Look here . . . " began Rick.

At that moment Mulheim made a desperate plunge towards Lydia. But she was too quick for him, and with a ruthlessness which she had always shown in her dealings throughout her life, she shot him. There was a deafening report. A scream from Gay.

When the smoke cleared away, the body of Kurt Mulheim sprawled grotesquely on the floor. Lydia moved forward and prodded him with the tip of her small foot.

"He's quite dead," she said.

"Are you a woman or a fiend?" Rick asked in horror.

She put away her revolver and smiled.

"I had to do it, and in any case do you see anything to grieve for in the death of that scum?"

"I admit that he's scum," said Rick. "But you're not much better yourself."

She winced.

"There was a time when you broke your heart for love of me, Rick," she said gently.

Rick looked at Gay. Overcome by what she had just witnessed, she had sunk into a chair weakly, and put her head in her hands. With yearning, he looked at the fair, bent young head. The whole affair seemed to him so monstrous. But one thing was very clear to him. England was at war with Germany. The sooner he got back there and joined up, the better. And Gay must go with him, as his wife.

But there was still this woman, Lydia. This public danger, this menace to decent society. What had she up her sleeve? What was she going to do next?

He said:

"Well, Lydia, the gloves are off on both sides. Now how do we stand?"

"Not quite where I wish to stand with you, Rick. I shall never rest until you grow to love me again."

"Then you will never rest," said Rick with a cracked laugh.

The angry blood stung her cheeks. She passed a look of loathing at Gay.

"Still hoping to mend a broken heart in the arms of Miss Burnett?"

"Since you put it that way," said Rick coldly.

Gay's head lifted. With all her heart she responded to those words and to the full meaning behind them. She said:

"Surely there can be an end now to all this horror. Can't we all get back to civilization and be sane again?"

"I have every intention of returning to civilization and taking Rick with me," said Lydia. "But you, my dear, I'm afraid must stay where you are. I have an aeroplane waiting. It arrived a few minutes ago in answer to my cable. It shall take Rick and myself to Cape Town. From there we shall get a German boat which will take us to Hamburg and — "

"Don't waste your time talking," interrupted Rick.

Lydia sighed. Taking a cigarette from her case, she lit it and smoked coolly, regarding him with those incredibly lovely eyes. She did not look twice at the body of the man whom she had just shot down in cold blood. She said:

"It is a pity that I have to do things by force. I would so much rather be friends with you, Rick. But you see, my dear, you leave me no choice. If you won't accompany me to Germany willingly, you must go as, shall we call it, a prisoner of war."

"You'll never get away with it. Do you think I'll sit beside you like a lamb and be removed by you to your infernal country?"

"No," said Lydia, "you will have to go as a sick, *very* sick, relative of mine. I have passports. For the time being we are American, and it will be easy for us to go wherever we wish with American passports."

Rick looked at her grimly.

"I'm not so sick as all that."

"But you are," she said sweetly. "Or at least you will be, shall I put it, so doped that you can make no protest."

Gay watched her, fascinated, and saw her lift from her bag something that gleamed in the light. A hypodermic syringe. Gay screamed and immediately Lydia gave orders for the natives behind her to hold her back. Gay said wildly:

"Don't do that to him. Don't put that stuff in him. God, how can you be so wicked? . . . "

"I'm afraid I can't waste time arguing with you," said Lydia. "When we've gone, you'll remain here, and I dare say old Greta will see that you never get out in order to tell the story."

"You *are* a fiend," said Rick.

She ignored Gay, who was screaming, the long-drawn, hopeless wail of one who has been driven beyond the limits of endurance. Rick Morrell's face was ghastly. The sweat poured down his face. As Lydia approached him, he poured abuse upon her. He said things which he would never have believed he could say to any woman. He would, in that moment, willingly have put his hands round that slim white throat of hers and strangled her. She knew it. But she was past caring. It seemed frightful to him that she should still look so angelically lovely. Her long-lashed eyes smiled at him while she drove the sharp point of the hypodermic with skill and precision into the firm brown flesh of his forearm.

"Fiend!" he shouted.

"Dear Rick," she murmured, "this will make you, oh, so much calmer!"

Agonizedly he looked over her head at Gay. She had ceased screaming. She had passed from hysteria into unconsciousness. She lay on the floor, still and piteous, and he could only look at her, straining desperately and futilely against the bonds that kept him from reaching her.

And after that, the white glare of the room began to grow dark, and his heart knocked strangely, and there was a singing in his ears. He cursed impotently, knowing that whatever drug Lydia had jabbed into his veins was taking effect.

He began to mutter incoherent things. He saw, as through a haze, Lydia's face. She seemed compassionate. He heard her voice:

"Poor Ricky. You must be my sick brother . . . just for a bit . . . until we get out of Africa. Then, when we are in Germany, you will be of the greatest help. You will start to draw all those beautiful, clever plans you used to draw when you were an engineer. We will do much together, you and I, and you will be thanked by my Fuehrer. He will forget the fact that you are English and you will love me just as you used to. Eh?"

He tried to answer, to curse her. He could not speak. The world was spinning about him. Hopelessly he fought against the dope, but it beat him. He gave a last despairing look at Gay's prostrate figure. After that he knew nothing. He realized, vaguely, that he was being taken out of the room, between two natives. He walked, unsteadily, with them, following Lydia to a waiting car. He had neither the mental nor physical strength left to resist. He was like a mental defective in their hands.

Gay did not move. She had at last reached a state of complete collapse. She did not even know that the man she loved so much had been taken from her, and that she was left alone.

19

DR. ISRAEL ISAACSON of Ligati lay half asleep in his hammock which was stretched on the north side of the verandah, protected as far as possible from the heat of the afternoon. Beside him a young native girl waved a large fan, keeping the flies away from him. When she stopped, he opened one eye and cursed her, whereupon she showed her white teeth in a grin and recommenced the rhythmic swaying of the fan.

Dr. Isaacson was in that state of dreaming as he dozed, and yet not dreaming; conscious of many unpleasant things which now and then caused his features to twitch and a groan to escape his lips.

His was a face typical of his race. Hook-nosed, shrewd, clever, with a small black-pointed beard, and a mass of black curly hair.

Israel Isaacson had lived all his life in

South Africa. He was a British subject and had a British passport. His father had been a Jewish doctor in the Cape. His mother a Cape woman. Fortunately for Israel, he had inherited his father's brains and most of his physical characteristics. There was nothing of the Negro in him except his over-thick lips and the colour of his nails.

He had followed in the footsteps of his father, and taken a degree. For some years he had practised medicine quite successfully in Liberia. Then too much drink and a variety of dark-skinned mistresses had dulled what was originally a good brain. He went from bad to worse and found himself, finally, doctoring natives instead of whites. In Ligati he was the only medical man available. But he had taken on a kind of travelling practice. He had an ancient Ford in which he drove for hundreds of miles round the wild, fierce countryside, attending patients in the outlying districts. His work ranged from curing natives of posionous snake-bite to attending women in difficult child-birth.

He was a genial fell , whether drunk

or sober, and popular. He was liked by the Europeans who crossed his path, and the only man for many miles around whom the British police trusted. "Mad Israel" they called him. But he knew a thing or two and they liked him.

Only last night, two very important pieces of news had been brought to him by a native runner from the nearest wireless station. One, that Great Britain was at war with Germany. The other that two British policemen from Liberia had been found murdered on the road between the coastal town and Ligati.

The murder of the policemen was of less importance to Israel Isaacson than the news of war. Jew that he was, he shared the antipathy of his race towards Adolf Hitler. He had read of the Jew-baiting in Nazi Germany. The concentration camps. The tortures. Dr. Isaacson did not relish the news of the war. There were many Germans in this part of Africa. He had stayed sober last night, thinking things out, wondering whether he would be advised to pack up and leave for the Cape and find himself in a more protected area.

The sound of a commotion, of voices outside the bungalow, roused him. He opened his eyes.

"What is all this?" he asked the girl irritably.

She shrugged her shoulders. She did not know.

"Go and see, woman," he ordered.

She obeyed. When she returned, her big liquid eyes were sparkling.

"White lady come here," she announced with excitement. "White lady dressed like boy."

Dr. Isaacson slid from his hammock and shook the sleep from his eyes. God, he was hot! He needed a bath. He wondered what the devil his girl was talking about. White ladies never came to Ligati. Mami was crazy.

A moment later he knew that Mami was right. He faced a slim, fair-haired English girl in his darkened sitting-room, and wondered if *he* was crazy, for he was hearing one of the most fantastic stories he had ever listened to in his life. He knew that strange things happened in Africa. He could tell some pretty queer stories, himself. But this girl, who said her name was Gay Burnett, told the strangest of them all.

He could see that she was ill, in a state of nervous exhaustion. The doctor in him became alert. He made her sit down, poured her out a dose from his medicine-chest and waited while she drank it before he questioned her further. The stimulant brought a tinge of colour to Gay's death-white cheeks. She began to talk again. And while he listened, Israel Isaacson thanked heaven that he was stone-cold sober today, and that he had not indulged in his usual orgy last night. He was in a state when he could deal with the matter intelligently.

From what he could gather, this girl had escaped an hour ago from old Greta's bungalow. Yes, he knew Greta. Wicked old rascal, he said. Would accept bribes from anybody. Well, after this German spy, Lydia Milcroft, had taken Rick away, Gay had been very ill for some hours, she told him. Greta had given her water and left her to herself. All last night she had lain in a stupor, too weak to move, believing that she was going to die. With the dawn she had recovered enough strength to get off her bed and climb through that window in which she had filed the bars. Greta had not noticed the loosened bars. Gay had escaped early this morning, but it took her hours to get here, to this bungalow. She could only walk a little way at a time, then had to sit down and recover her strength.

"Rick told me your name," Gay finished her story. "He had meant to get you to help us both. He had been told your address by the police. I asked any native I met, as I walked. I just said: 'White doctor, Isaacson . . . ', kept repeating it. They knew."

"Yes, they all know me," said Isaacson.

Gay looked at him dully. She was thankful to God to be sitting here in the bungalow of a man who spoke perfect English and seemed reliable. After all that she had been through, all the horrors, the mental torture, the treachery of people like Mulheim and Lydia, it was heaven to find herself in the hands of a man whom the British police recommended.

"We've got to save Mr. Morrell," she

said. "Oh, Dr. Isaacson, we've *got* to save him."

"There, there, don't worry. We will," he reassured her kindly. "Now, you say he was doped . . . that the woman had a 'plane waiting?"

"Yes. And she put a hypodermic needle in his arm. I saw it just before I fainted. She was going to pass him off as her invalid brother. She had two American passports."

"Very clever," said Isaacson, rubbing his hands. "Very clever, my dear Miss Burnett. But Israel Isaacson will outwit her. The lady is German, you say?"

"Of German extraction, although you would think her English, and she married an American so has an American passport."

"But she works for Germany."

"Yes, like Kurt Mulheim." Gay shuddered in every limb as she thought of the man whom Lydia had murdered before her very eyes.

Into the doctor's eyes there came a steely spark.

"I am a Jew, as you can see," he said softly. "I have no love for Germans. They have tortured my people. If they got hold of me, they would do likewise. If I can help England in this war, I shall do so."

"Yes, yes," said Gay. "But it is Mr. Morrell we must save before it is too late."

"We will manage, somehow," said Isaacson.

In an agony of anxiety she looked at him.

"Mrs. Milcroft is so clever. She has money. She will get that 'plane to the coast before we can get there."

"There is always wireless, my dear young lady."

"Can you get a message to the police . . . stop the 'plane at the aerodrome?"

"Undoubtedly. They cannot have reached the Cape yet. They will not risk night-flying. They will have stopped last night, en route."

The tears began to stream down Gay's face. She was broken in mind and spirit. Her courage had been so sorely taxed and she felt weak and ill.

"I must leave it all to you, Dr. Isaacson," she whispered. "I only beg you, for God's sake, to be quick."

He patted her hand.

"Don't worry. No need for tears. You shall rest here while I do what is necessary."

She looked up at him with eyes wide with terror.

"Don't leave me alone. I can never bear to be left alone again. They'll get me . . . Lydia Milcroft's spies . . . or that Chinaman from Quoon . . . for God's sake don't leave me, Dr. Isaacson."

He clicked his tongue against his teeth. The poor child, what she had gone through! he thought. Enough to send a strong-minded man out of his head. But she was still brave enough to think of this man, whom she loved. She would still be willing to go with him, Isaacson, and take risks for her lover's sake. He felt a great admiration for her courage, coupled with intense pity. He thought, too, with pleasure, that if he saved her, he would serve the English. And if he defeated Lydia Milcroft, he would defeat a part of Germany, of that man, Hitler, whom he loathed with all his Jewish soul.

"I won't leave you, Miss Burnett," he said. "I go only to send my runner to

265

the radio-station with a message that will stop that woman from leaving the shores of Africa. But you must remember that you are ill. You do not want to pass out completely before you get to Mr. Morrell, eh?"

Gay wiped away her tears and smiled faintly. The first smile for long weeks.

"No, I don't want to do that."

"Then lie still and rest until I return. Then we shall take my car and go to the nearest police-station. That will be a long tiring drive and you will need all your own strength, as well as my medicine, to help you through."

She nodded. Hope, the first real, burning hope that she had known for a long time, surged through her. Already her weakness was passing. She could bear more, yes, anything, if she really thought that Rick could be saved, and that they could both get back to England again.

She lay back in her chair with closed eyes. Dr. Isaacson sent his girl in with food and drink. Then he went to his desk and, with an excitement which he, personally, had not felt for years, wrote an urgent message for his friend, the wireless operator, and gave it to the fastest cross-country runner in Ligati.

Some hours later Gay, still very weak with fever and exhaustion, sat beside the doctor, driving down the sunlit dusty road that led out of Ligati, back towards the coast.

Her hopes ran even higher now. The message had been given to the wireless station and flashed to the police. The answer had been delivered to Dr. Isaacson. The German spy, Lydia Milcroft, and her 'sick brother', would be held in custody when they landed at the Cape until Gay arrived to give her evidence.

It seemed to Gay much too long before she could reach civilization, and feel really and truly safe again. Only the Jewish doctor, himself, knew the strain that was put on her feeble resistance. He gave her what help he could with strong drugs. But it was a very white, shaky, frail Gay who came at the end of that long journey face to face with Rick and Lydia again.

The meeting took place in a police-station near the aerodrome where Lydia's pilot had landed the 'plane that previous day. Lydia had raved and ranted in vain, when she had been detained and prevented from continuing her journey to Hamburg.

"I am an American subject," she had declared furiously. "My brother and I demand to see the American Consul."

Her 'brother', she was told, was not in a fit condition to see anybody. When Lydia declared that he was a mental defective, she was told, drily, that the doctor who had examined Rick had other views. In his opinion, Mr. Morrell was merely suffering from the effects of a drug, and until he had recovered from it and could speak for himself, the authorities were not prepared to listen to Mrs. Milcroft's explanations.

The moment that Lydia heard that Rick was in medical hands, she knew the game was up. He would be given an antidote for the drug and by the morning he would be able to speak for himself. This, then, was the end. And she knew that it was still more the end, once she was informed that a Miss Gay Burnett was on her way here to give evidence.

So Gay had escaped from old Greta and found help! A hundred times that day Lydia gnashed her teeth with rage and cursed herself for not having finished Gay off, as she had finished Mulheim.

So came the hour of reckoning.

Rick Morrell, weak and shaky but himself again, told the police everything. When Gay arrived, with Dr. Isaacson, she endorsed and completed the story. Lydia Milcroft did not stand a chance, and she knew it. But she was callous to the end. She sneered at Gay. She smiled at Rick. She gave the men who had interrogated her one of her most disarming smiles.

"Such a pity that I did not destroy *all* the evidence," she said, with a wicked look at Gay. "Then I might have got away with it. Oh, well, they shoot spies, don't they? I shall hate being shot. But I regret nothing that I have done. *Heil Hitler!*"

There was dead silence as she was led away. The police authorities were staggered by the revelations which had been unfolded to them that day. There was no pity in the hearts of any of them for the beautiful woman spy who had behaved with such utter callousness, and betrayed the country which had sheltered her, with such ruthless lack of scruple.

And Rick and Gay had neither eyes nor ears for anybody save themselves. Mad with joy and relief, they clung to each other. Both of them ill, shaken, almost at the end of their tether, they were strong enough in this hour to feel all the rapture of their reunion, and of knowing that their troubles were ended. These two who had been so near to death experienced the peculiar thrill of realization that the gates of life were once more open wide to them . . . rich with promise.

"You saved me, my darling. I owe my release to you," Rick said, holding Gay's slim young figure close to him, his lips warm and eager upon her upturned face.

She said:

"Oh, Rick, Rick my darling . . . I might have lost you for ever. This is too good to be true."

"It is true, darling. You need never be afraid of anything, of anybody again. I am going to take you back to England as soon as we can get a boat. As soon as I've cleared up my affairs. Thank God I have enough money for our fare and to keep us going until I'm in the Army."

She trembled and strained closer to him.

"Oh, I don't want to think of war . . . of anything . . . that might take you from me again."

"Don't worry, dear," he whispered back, stroking her hair. "Forget everything now that is unpleasant. Just be happy with me. We shall have many long weeks together as man and wife, before you need talk of losing me."

She gave a deep sigh and closed her eyes. She heard Dr. Isaacson's voice:

"I must congratulate you, Mr. Morrell, on your escape. I am proud to have been of help to the brave young lady who is, I presume, your fiancée."

"That is so," said Rick; "and we owe a lot to you, Dr. Isaacson."

"I am English," said the doctor with pathetic pride.

They shook hands. The next moment the room was filling up with newspaper reporters . . . eager for the biggest spy story, the greatest thrill, they had had for years. And there was a secret slave market in it, too. Gay Burnett and Rick Morrell were going to be front-page news. And the West African newspapers were willing to pay a good price for that story. As much of it as Miss Burnett and Mr. Morrell cared to tell. They needn't worry about money. It was theirs for the taking. . . . It was a bit of luck in the eyes of the reporters, getting a story like this right on top of the declaration of war.

★ ★ ★

One month later, Gay sat in a long chair, with a rug across her knees, on the deck of a homeward-bound liner.

She was alone for the moment. Rick had gone down to their cabin to fetch a book. Gay felt pleasantly lazy . . . neither reading nor knitting, like most of the women who were on deck. Everybody seemed to be supplied with large quantities of khaki wool. Gay had bought hers, too. Rick would need a pullover and a scarf and socks before he reached England. But she wanted to do nothing for a bit. Just to lie and dream and rejoice, and feel that gorgeous sense of peace and happiness which had been hers in full measure since she left Africa.

They had been a week out at sea. The weather was still warm and lovely, and so far they had had a calm voyage. Even the seven short days of sea-breezes and plenty of sleep and good food and, last but not least, Rick's tender care and devotion, had made a different person of Gay. She was putting on weight. Her cheeks had filled out. Her eyes were no longer fear-haunted. They were tranquil and unafraid.

She had so much that was pleasant to think about now. She endeavoured never to let her mind slip back for a single instant to those horrors through which she and Rick had passed. The fever-ridden jungle, the desert, the gilded prison of Quoon, Li Matin, and the ghastly slave market . . . all were phantoms of the past. It all seemed almost unbelievable now . . . as though it had never happened. And she need not even remember the misery of being an unsuccessful film-actress in

Liberia . . . those awful early days with Kurt Mulheim. Nor her lonely struggles in London after the death of Cousin Gladys. For she was Mrs. Morrell now, Rick's wife. They had been married by special licence in Cape Town, soon after Rick's rescue from the hands of Lydia.

Their honeymoon — a week at a lovely English hotel with a flower-filled garden leading down to the sea — had been a revelation of never-ending delight to both Gay and Rick. They had much to discover in each other, for they really knew each other so little. But they soon discovered that their marriage was going to be a phenomenal success. Every hour, every day drew them nearer, dearer. At the end of that week's glorious honeymoon, Gay knew herself to be utterly in love with her husband, and unutterably loved by him.

By the time the newspapers had finished with them, they had both of them earned more than enough to pay the heavy fare back to England, so that set them financially on their feet. They realized it must, inevitably, be a struggle when they got home. But they were prepared to face it, with and for each other. Rick would join the Army at once, and Gay meant to get her Red Cross Certificate, and work at some kind of civil job until she was called up.

Money — or the lack of it — did not worry her. It never had done so. She had been poor enough in all conscience in those early days in the Cotswolds in her grandfather's home. But what was very necessary to Gay's heart was love . . . and love she had now in plenty. A glorious, passionate love such as she had never dared hope for before she met Rick Morrell.

Rick had bought her a small but much-needed trouseau in Cape Town. She did not think she was as smartly or expensively dressed as some of the women travelling first-class on this boat, but Rick said she looked every bit as attractive, and much more so. Today she was a sleek, well-groomed young woman in her blue and white linen suit, her gay scarf, her fair curls charmingly coiffured by the ship's hairdresser, her skin, which had grown dry and harsh after the weeks of neglect in the wilds of Africa, fast recovering and looking smooth, satin-soft, healthily pink again.

A girl of her own age, also travelling with her husband back to England, strolled past Gay's chair and stopped to say a few words.

"Feeling better today, Mrs. Morrell?"

Gay, who was still thrilled by the sound of that newly acquired name, smiled and nodded.

"Tons better, thanks Mrs. Lawson."

Diana Lawson sat at their table in the dining-saloon. She was a pretty thing, but discontented looking, and invariably full of grievances. Rick had no use for her.

"She doesn't know when she's well off," had been his comment on Mrs. Lawson. "I'd like to see her come through the hell you endured in Africa, and still be sweet and smiling."

Today Diana had fresh troubles.

"I'm just terrified this trip. The news from England is so awful. Those vile Germans! They've sunk a ship called the *Athenia*. We might be mined or torpedoed. Do you realize that?"

"Yes, it's possible, but not probable," said Gay with another smile. "And I don't waste any sleep thinking about it.

I expect we'll get back quite safely."

"Nothing seems to bother *you*," Diana sniffed, and passed on.

Gay shut her eyes and leaned back against the cushion. Naturally, she thought, a girl like Diana Lawson, who had lived a normal, sheltered existence, could never possibly know life as she, Gay, knew it. Never understand that what Gay had passed through in Africa was so awful that it had left her without fear of anything . . . even a grim thing like being mined or torpedoed. Death, if death through such a disaster should overtake her, would seem kind compared with the fate that had awaited her, only a few weeks ago, in the hands of the Chinese ruler of Quoon.

Suddenly she began to tremble, convulsively. She seemed to see the Chinaman's yellow, mask-like face. That strange exotic garden . . . the heavy satin robes weighing her down . . . the hot interminable hours of waiting . . . the sight of Rick stumbling in the chain-gang. A phantasy of horror . . . And when it passed, another came in its place . . . the great market square of Ligati . . . the sound of the gong as each slave girl was sold. The merciless, lovely face of Lydia Milcroft . . . the sight of the hypodermic needle going into Rick's arm . . . the dead, sprawling body of Kurt Mulheim.

Black, nameless, unmentionable things . . . best forgotten for ever.

Gay buried her face in her hands. When she had these lapses, she shivered uncontrollably until Rick's arms, Rick's kisses drove memory from her mind and brought her back to the poignant sweetness of the present.

She felt a touch on her bent head. Looking up, she saw Rick. And at once her fears dissolved like dew in the strong sunlight. She put up her hand and caught his, and drew it against her cheek. Her darling husband! A Rick almost unrecognizable from the one she had first met in an African garden. That Rick who had been drink-sodden, going fast and furious to the devil. This was a clean, sane, and very sober Rick who looked the picture of health and most attractive in his grey flannels, his white tennis shirt, a silk handkerchief knotted around his brown neck. This was a

Rick who, with a pipe in the corner of his mouth, looked with clear and contented eyes upon the world, knowing that those black demons of his would never resurrect; that the young fool who had almost ruined body and soul for a worthless woman, had become a sane man who had learnt his lesson; and was husband to the sweetest and bravest girl he had ever met.

At the moment, those handsome blue eyes of his were looking at Gay with grave concern.

"Sweet, you're not ill?"

She laughed. Her cheeks were rose-red under the golden tan and her eyes brilliant and fearless again.

"No, no. Just a sudden bad spell . . . you know how I sometimes think . . . "

Rick put the pipe in his pocket, laid down his book and sat on her chair, putting an arm about her slight shoulders.

"Don't think, darling. I've told you not to. Just be happy and remember that I adore you."

"That's something worth remembering," she said, with a blissful sigh.

"Has anybody done anything to upset you?"

"No. Only something Diana Lawson said about being scared of the Germans torpedoing our boat made me think of all the horrors we've been through. I don't feel this war will frighten me so far as my own personal danger is concerned. If I have any fears they are for you!"

He caressed the fair curls lightly with one hand and with the other lifted her fingers to his lips.

"I shall be all right. I'll come through. I feel it. And as for the boat being torpedoed — there may be a slight risk, but even if we did strike a mine or something of the sort, it doesn't necessarily mean that we'd all go to our deaths. Anyhow, that Lawson girl is a menace. If there were not a war on, she'd find something else to upset her. But I won't have her upsetting *you*."

Gay laughed. All her happiness and self-confidence had returned. Feeling at peace with the world, she sat back in the curve of her husband's arm and watched the sun sparkle on the blue-green water.

A steward rushed up to them excitedly.

"Convoy just passing, sir, astern. You can see it round the other side. A British cruiser . . . worth seeing, sir . . . "

Rick looked down at his wife.

"Want to stay here, sweet?"

"No let's go and see the cruiser."

They stood together with a rapidly increasing crowd of passengers watching the convoy pass on its way. Somehow the sight of that slim grey cruiser cutting through the radiant water, flying the British flag, gave Gay a sense of terrific pride and patriotism. And it brought home acutely the fact that England *was* at war.

She had a sudden vision of Rick in a khaki uniform and herself as a soldier's wife. Together they would do what they could for England and help erase Nazism — that sinister ugly blot — from the pages of civilization. It must be death not only to Lydia Milcroft and Kurt Mulheim . . . but to every other Nazi who threatened the peace and freedom of the English nation.

From the saloon came the strains of music. Somebody was playing a march. Yes, soon there would be men marching,

marching, in every corner of the British Empire, and Rick would march with them.

Gay pressed his arm tightly to her side. But she was no longer afraid. He would come through . . . He had said it and she felt that it was so.

The graceful cruiser steamed away into the golden haze of the distance. The passengers dispersed. Rick and Gay were alone.

As though by mutual consent, they turned to each other and embraced, passionately.

THE END